D0363853

THE LAST ROMANTIC
OUT OF BELFAST

THE LAST ROMANTIC
OUT OF BELFAST

Sam Keery

Book Guild Publishing

Sussex, England

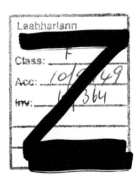

This edition published in Great Britain in 2011 by
The Book Guild Ltd
Pavilion View
19 New Road
Brighton, BN1 1UF

First published in 1984 by The Blackstaff Press

Typesetting in Baskerville by
Keyboard Services, Luton, Bedfordshire

Printed in Great Britain by
CPI Antony Rowe

A catalogue record for this book is available from
The British Library

ISBN 978 1 84624 579 4

1

First there was coming out of darkness into light. The darkness was night and the light was the light of street lamps, but only at the corner as they turned it, his father and he, he riding drowsy in his father's arms against his shoulder, the street empty, dark and silent except just there where the lamps shone. He was nearly asleep but still clutching very tightly a beautiful doll that was not his, to which he had no right. He must have seized the doll somewhere back in the darkness out of which they had come and he feared that she would be taken from him when his grip was loosened by sleep, and sleep lay in wait for him on all sides around the pool of yellow lamplight through which they briefly passed. The light shone on the blank iron-railed window of a large building on which night had long settled. He hugged the beautiful doll to him very hard as they stepped for a moment or two into the light, his father and he, before they were swallowed up again by oblivion.

He raced home from school each day and went first to a little fish he had in a jampot. The fish was listless and they said it would die. When he came out of school he would look backwards as the school dwindled away behind him, like the receding memory of an unhappy event that would never recur. He would put down the jampot on the street and put far from him the thought of school and of tomorrow. Tomorrow would never come. Every

1

day after school he believed that tomorrow would never come. It was simply a question of faith. If he believed it hard enough it would be so. That was his secret which he would not tell though the teachers came and looked at him and conferred in low voices. The street was quiet and peaceful and he set down his fish in the middle of the road and he was at peace. It would always be like that. It would always be after school on the quiet street, glistening softly after rain, under a gentle sky of low clouds that spread over all its mantle soft and grey.

Week by week he followed eagerly the adventures of a boy in his comics. One week he turned the tables on a gang of wicked half-castes with the help of a unique weapon of marvellous power. It was not the picture which impressed him so vividly as its name. It was the fascinating name the weapon was called which seemed to him to contain the secret of its power to rout enemies. For a little while he kept to himself his delight in this wonderful new word until he felt compelled to share it, if only to let the others see that he had taken its mystery to his heart unaided. Shyly but proudly he held out the page for them to see and uttered the name.

The others were older. They had comics he was too young for. He longed for their approval. He felt sure that in some way he had passed one of their tests.

'A what?' they asked him incredulously. Their voices were full of scorn. Where had he gone wrong? In dismay he scanned again the word whose contemplation had given him so much pleasure.

'A *matchyne* gun,' he repeated, giving the word the pronunciation he had chosen for it but realising now in a flash of understanding that came as he listened, as they would listen, to the sound he had invented for it, that it was not so. He suddenly knew what they would say. He had been a fool.

'A machine gun,' they said impatiently, correcting his error with contempt. Of course. He crept away in disgrace. Once more he had fallen into the trap of having fancies on encountering the printed form of a familiar and commonplace word.

He swapped his comics with his friend Victor who lived up an entry near the mill. One day when he went to Victor's house it was crowded with neighbours in an excited and expectant mood. His friend did not seem pleased to see him, nor that so many of the neighbours were there. They had to squeeze up to make room for him. He got the impression that his friend had some unfinished matter to attend to before coming out to play and swap comics, and that the presence of so many people was interfering with this.

His friend's mother was seated on a tall high-backed armchair like a throne, laughing and talking with the people gathered round her. His friend stood sullenly at her side trying to wheedle something out of her. He kept nudging and whining at her to wear her down and pulling at her as if to draw her away.

For a while she ignored him. Then she turned to him and challenged him to tell the people what it was he wanted. This appeared not to suit him at all and he pulled and whined at her even more. Was it money his friend was after? He thought Victor was trying to pull his mother towards wherever she kept her purse.

'I will,' she promised him, 'I will if you tell them what it is you're after.'

He thought it was money for some fool thing that Victor was after, that the people would laugh at him for wanting.

But all of a sudden Victor's mother undid the top of her dress and out flopped her breast, a startling and a thrilling sight.

'That's what it is he's after,' she announced to the people with a rueful smile. The people laughed. One of them clapped her hands. His friend Victor cried bitterly. He stamped his feet in rage and shame as his mother revealed, for all to see, the secret of his private consolation.

His father's workshop first raised for him a problem that he never solved. It seemed so easy when it first came to him as he lay drowsy in bed just before sleep. What, he wondered, does the workshop look like now, with nobody looking at it, all silent, empty, and dark except for the streetlamp outside. It was not that he had any wish to go and look because that would not have answered his question which was: what does it look like when *nobody* is looking at it? Moreover, he realised, it was nothing to do with night or day, light or dark. He would lie in bed on the edge of sleep and try to imagine what his father's workshop looked like *unseen*. Night after night, mentally he would travel to the door. He would try to imagine throwing open the door suddenly, to try to capture the instant of seeing. But no matter how quick he fancied doing that, it was not quick enough. The things in the workshop *assumed their forms at the moment of being observed*: the great bench, the sewing machine, the electric rasps, the heaps of lasts and the sheets of leather. But what of that other mysterious form, the one they had the moment before?

He took the problem to his father one day as his father sat on his shoemaker's stool, sewing on a sole. He asked his father what things looked like when nobody is looking at them. The same as when they are looking at them, his father said. But what way is that, he asked his father, trying to get him to see that it raised a baffling problem, one aspect of which – though not the only one – was the *point of view*: is it the way they look from one side or the other or all sides at once? One night when he lay in bed he thought he caught a glimpse of an answer and it frightened him so that he had cried out in fear: perhaps things not being looked at *did not exist*. Perhaps he should have framed the question to his father in a theological form: *what does God see?* As it was his father could throw no light on it.

'I hope,' his father said gravely, 'you don't talk that way at school.'

Of course he did not. How could his father think him such a fool? He stayed to watch his father make the twist he sewed with from strands of white thread which were vigorously waxed and pointed with a pig's whisker. The pigs' whiskers were in little boxes; wax comes in long sticks like chocolate. The sticks of wax soon turn into balls from the warmth of the hand. Little balls of wax lay everywhere. They were cut with deep grooves from stroking the twist and upon their surfaces there was a fine clear network of lines like the veins upon a leaf which was the imprint of his father's palm.

The pig's whisker was fixed to the twist in an operation of great dexterity combining spit, wax, and a roll against his father's wax-stained apron that he loved to see.

'All the fun of the fair,' his father announced importantly as if upon a stage, 'the quickness of the hand deceives the eye. Performed before the Crown Heads of Europe. Latecomers not admitted after the curtain rises.'

He dreamt he saw the heavenly host over the school playground. There was the playground, silent and empty with the blackstone wall around it; the cemetery, though for Catholics, on the other side; then the mill and the blue hills beyond. It was broad daylight and the heavenly host was pale and faint against the clouds. On and on they came, white-robed, serene, some bearded, row upon row, rank upon rank, for ever and ever, world without end, Amen. He was not at first alarmed and gazed at them calmly as they floated by between the two school chimneys.

Then something about them stirred a feeling of uneasiness and it began to grow. It was a little like when he was having his nightmare. In his nightmare he would be playing happily on the Boiling Well Meadow, which seemed to stretch away to the horizon. On the horizon there would appear something small and dark that was not a cloud but something far more sinister and it would grow and grow, racing rapidly across the sky as it grew, so that he had to shout himself awake before that awful dark thing enveloped him forever.

But there was no darkness in his dream of heaven. What began to grow was inside him; it was nothing less than the awful meaning of eternity. He fixed his gaze on one tall benign figure only just brighter than the bright sky and realized that *he would never end*. He saw horizon follow horizon in infinite succession each containing all the time there had ever been and more. The heavenly host would go on and on for ever and ever without respite or peace or final rest. It was intolerable. He cried out in fear at such an awful doom.

They wakened him and told him he was dreaming. Was it your nightmare, his father asked, and he told his father no, it was not.

'It was heaven,' he said, and tried to convey to them the horror of neverendingness, of foreverandeverness, 'heaven is far too long'.

He would be calmed only by the reassurance that somewhere there was an end, however far.

For a little while he was famous as the boy who did not want to go to heaven.

Now that he was not going to go, they said, would he

give his ticket to somebody else? For, they told him solemnly, trying to keep from laughing, an awful lot of people in Belfast would like to go but wouldn't be able to. Did he know that a lot of Belfast people would not be able to go? He said no, he did not, and they all laughed. They told each other it was not fair to laugh, God help him, but went on laughing just the same.

He saw little glasses of a golden liquid being insinuated confidentially into people's hands in his grandmother's parlour. The people whispered shocked protests but gave way because of the occasion. He caught the smell of what was in the little glasses. It was a very serious smell. It always chastened him into seriousness when it came at him in a gust through the doorways of the public houses, mingled with loud voices, brutal and excited. His young aunt had one of the glasses and for amusement gave him a tiny sip. He spat it out in revulsion and they all laughed, though they told her to be careful not to make him sick. They don't like it at that age, they said, and are easy made sick. The hot sweet sour fumes were very sickly and he shuddered. They laughed at his bewilderment at how they could drink such stuff.

The soldier smiled too. He was a guardsman though not just then in his scarlet uniform. He had watched the guardsman sit cross-legged, shining his silver buttons, in the bedroom that had the framed text saying *I am Alpha and Omega, the beginning and the ending, saith the Lord.* The soldier sat on the arm of the couch in an attitude of casual gracefulness and his young aunt sat beside him. There was talk of India and Windsor Palace that filled him with intense longings. One of his uncles sang 'Oh play to me Gypsy' and another sang 'When the blue of the night' just like it was sung on the wireless.

If only I could see her,
Oh, how happy would I be!
Where the blue of the night
Meets the gold of the day
Some-one waits for me.

The soldier also sang. His song was 'Empty saddles in the old corral'. It touched the boy to the heart. He thought enviously how wonderful it must be to touch people's hearts as his was touched, to be admired the way he was admiring the soldier singer. He exulted in a vision of himself playing a heroic tragic part, on horseback, in ill-fated enterprises noble but doomed, watched by all the people in the room, but above all by the handsome soldier, all deeply moved. He was filled with beautiful heartbreaking images of empty saddles and riderless horses, whether made so by war or by time.

The soldier raised his arm behind his head to lean on it. To the boy's dismay there was a horrid place under the soldier's arm bleached by sweat. He tried his hardest not to feel disgust. He turned away from the awful thought that his hero was stained and debased, though a taint of corruption remained in his mind the whole evening.

That night he dreamed of being carried on the guardsman's shoulder. The guardsman had on his scarlet tunic and all around them was the murmur of people. The sweat stain under his arm was yellow and could not be hidden. But his splendour, though marred, was still magnificent, still imperial, still praetorian, as he raised him to his shoulder and carried him high through the admiring throng.

2

Hallowe'en was drawing near. Already as the evenings darkened some of the younger children began to put on the lurid Hallowe'en masks with the livid lips sodden from being shouted through, giving to their cries the taste of cardboard. They boasted of what squibs and rockets they had or had been promised.

It was toffee-apple time. In old Miss Williamson's shop the golden toffee-apples were laid out in glittering array. The children loved to bite into the two kinds of sweetness simultaneously: the one hard but bland, the other soft yet sharp. Old Miss Williamson would rap the tray smartly with her little silver hammer to separate the toffee-apples, each transfixed by a white stick. Sometimes the fresh green living apple was still faintly visible within its shining tomb of translucent gold.

The young McCabe child played with his brand new cap gun round the street lamp at old Miss Williamson's shop, holding it up to the light so he could admire its elegance. Bang! bang! he went with his new gun happily in the lamplight. Hallowe'en was near and soon there would be bigger bangs. Rockets would start to shoot up into the sky even before darkness fell, and shoals of masked excited children – confused by a festival which, unlike Christmas, did not start the moment they opened their eyes in the morning – would rush this way and that to where the rockets soared, asking is it now? is Hallowe'en now? Strange silent figures would flit about, emerging mysteriously from entries and doorways, black-faced, dark-robed, refusing to speak, vanishing abruptly before people could guess who they were and leaving in their wake a delicious thrill of fear that not quite all of them had been *real*. There would be nuts, there would be plum duff with a silver threepenny bit in it, there would be ghost stories round the fire. Hallowe'en was nearly upon them and already in the evenings the Spirit of Time Past was taking possession of the streets.

Constable Blake, his day's work done, enforcing the laws of the land, was wearily heading for home along the street which resounded with the cries of masked children, some of whom should undoubtedly have been in their beds. The children warily made way for his burly figure, partly because it was easier for them to get out of his way than he out of theirs, and partly because they would have been wary of him anyway, the young McCabe child as wary as the rest, if along with the rest he had seen Constable Blake in time. Insolence and bravado were not features of his disposition, which on the contrary inclined to the timid, and he would never have dreamed of letting off his cap gun, could he have avoided it, right in the path of a large policeman draped in a black rubbery-smelling greatcoat hanging open, equipped with a fearsome *real* black revolver with a black chain on it and with huge red hands that were cold and of a very rough texture. But rough only in texture, not in the way they held and handled him. Subsequent questioning firmly established that there had been no roughness whatsoever meted out to him, over and above what was strictly necessary to confiscate his cap gun. Constable Blake had leaned down over him in a manner which, if not completely identical to that in which a mother would attend to something about her child by feeling for it – for nobody but a mother can hit that action off to a T, least of all a stout policeman at the end of a busy day on his feet – nevertheless the manner of one well used to children, and had gently prised the little boy's fingers loose from his cap gun, which, after throwing back the greatcoat, he stowed away in a deep pocket. Constable Blake then proceeded on his way in a westerly direction, presumably that of home, and home too the McCabe child went in tears.

Had he been firing the gun in the man's face, his mother wanted to know.

Or maybe some of the other ones had, his Aunt Mary suggested.

What had the others been up to?

Who were all the other children?

Was he playing with the bad children again?

Were they knocking on people's doors and running away?

Were they putting squibs through people's letter boxes?

It wouldn't be well for him if he had been putting squibs through letter boxes!

But Mr McCabe interrupted them. Constable Blake was a man he had once made boots for and he rebuked the boy's mother and his aunts for doubting his story.

'Don't you women run away with the idea,' he said sternly, 'that Billy Blake wouldn't do a thing like that.' And he added grimly, 'the same bloody man'.

The women turned to him in consternation. What for, they demanded of him, what would he do a thing like that for? Robbing a child of its toy!

Mr McCabe answered them quite simply.

'To give to his own children,' he said sadly with a sigh, and the women fell silent. For a while no one spoke. What was there to say about such a sad truth?

After a while Mr Stuart remarked, in order to lift the gloom, that he had once fallen foul of the law himself years before. In fact, to commemorate the event, and to prove to people what a desperado he had been in times gone by, before he settled down and became law-abiding, he kept a yellow newspaper-clipping folded away among the insurance policies and licences for dog, shotgun and wireless tucked into a place at the top of the grandfather clock – behind its ear as it were. The newspaper clipping did indeed name him as defendant and stated briefly what direction he had been proceeding in when he was apprehended for riding a bicycle without lights and that the fine had been one shilling and sixpence, or, as Mr Stuart preferred to express it, eighteen pence.

Mr Stuart now produced this criminal record and put on his glasses to study it as if for the first time, after which he carefully folded it and put it away again into the safe keeping of the grandfather clock before he described what he called his arrest and subsequent trial.

This young bobby had come out at him from nowhere, he said, with his notebook at the ready. Mr Stuart pointed out to him that his lighting equipment was in perfect working order, front and rear. But the young bobby had, as Mr Stuart put it, trumped this ace with the words, 'Ah, but you didn't have them switched on.'

'Oh they know the law,' said Mr McCabe eagerly, 'the RUC men all have an exam to pass. Who they can charge, who they can't. That fella was out looking for summonses to fill the charge book.'

Mr Stuart related his entering the court-house and being spotted by this young bobby hanging about with a squad of others. His friendly demeanour had surprised Mr Stuart, considering the circumstances.

'He nodded at me,' said Mr Stuart, 'as if he was glad to see me and he whispers at me that he'll let me know when it's my turn.'

Mr Stuart cast about in his mind for an analogy that

would convey the obliging manner of the young bobby outside the courtroom.

'You know the way you would offer assistance to somebody gaping about them in a strange place. I had to stop myself thanking him,' said Mr Stuart. When his turn came the young bobby had escorted him into the courtroom to answer for his dreadful crime and steered him into the pulpit, whispering in his ear to say yes, just to say yes.

'When I was coming out of the dock after sentence was passed,' said Mr Stuart, omitting entirely any account of evidence given and weighed in the scales of justice which seemingly had left no impression whatsoever, and passing straight to the part which had impressed him very deeply, 'when I was leaving the dock this young bobby gave my arm a squeeze and told me that I *had done well*.'

'He meant,' pointed out Mr McCabe gravely, 'that you did well for *him*. Oh, Court Day is a big day for the RUC men.'

Mr Stuart repeated the words about doing well, just as the young bobby had spoken them, in a tone in which satisfaction was curiously mingled with relief and congratulation, and Mr McCabe offered to explain the importance that Court Day played in the lives of policemen. Mr McCabe could speak with authority on the subject. His side of the family had a big police connection and some were in the army, several had been in both, since men who had done service with the Irish Guards could be half an inch shorter than the regulation six foot for the Royal Ulster Constabulary. You would see them at funerals, big red-faced men that ran to beef, sitting squeezed up in parlours with their bowler hats on their knees and a glass of something to warm them, letting fall things about India, about Windsor Palace, about the Troubles and the Falls Road, in deep musical voices, for they were all singers too, but with tantalising reserve, for only Mr McCabe was passionate in his talk.

'That squad of them you mentioned,' cried Mr McCabe excitedly, referring to the bobbies hanging about the court-house on the day of Mr Stuart's trial, 'that squad were waiting to bring on their own cases and they would all have been biting their nails as nervous as performers waiting in the wings of a theatre.' Mr McCabe pronounced it thee-*ay*-ter.

But Mr Stuart objected that it was he who felt like a performer.

'I'm damned but I thought he was going to trot me round the courtroom like a bull at a show for them to give points,' he said.

There was some laughter at this, until Mr McCabe returned them to seriousness again by repeating very earnestly what a big day Court Day was for the RUC men.

'The younger men,' he told them sternly, 'like that young bobby of Tom's here, would all be on eggs for fear they were made a monkey of if they didn't watch their Ps and Qs.

'And,' he added grimly, 'some of the long service men as well.

'When they go into court,' expounded Mr McCabe, wagging his finger, 'all doubts have to be left at the door. Absolute certainty is the order of the day or else they'll be made a monkey of. It's a case of you swear his life away or he'll swear yours.'

The odd mixture of scorn, indignation and compassion that filled Mr McCabe's deep voice made his hearers unsure whether it was directed at accusers or accused, or fell equally on both. Mr Stuart studied Mr McCabe thoughtfully and puffed his pipe.

'And when there's an accident or a crime,' cried Mr McCabe, excited at the imparting of knowledge which

14

never ceased to be a source of wonder to him, and sitting very upright in his chair with both hands resting on his knees, 'when there's an accident or a crime, God help us all they have to draw it on paper with all the measurements in the minutest detail. Such drawing and rubbing out. Drawing and rubbing out.

'Up half the night,' he assured them solemnly, 'up half the night with the wife helping them and the children dare hardly speak.'

As to the getting of summonses, Mr McCabe decided to express the importance of this in the dramatic form by enacting a little charade. He appeared to be turning over the pages of some imaginary book, heavy and large, wetting a finger most realistically for the purpose and managing to convey by his stern face that he was miming someone in authority and that the book was important.

'Is that a Bible he's at or what is it?' whispered a neighbour woman in amusement, and though Mr McCabe did not let on he had heard her, nevertheless he thought it useful to explain in a little aside that it was in fact the police barracks charge-book. Resuming the mimed page-turning he began to speak in a rather bad middle-class accent, hard and sarcastic.

'Oh a very law-abiding class of persons you have round you here compared to some other localities if the summonses in this book is anything to go by. Oh you could sleep easy in your bed round here all night. Do the shops and banks have bolts on their doors at all or could they leave them on the jar? I wonder is it worth their while locking up premises at night, such law-abiding people about these parts.'

Mr McCabe spoke these words with such scathing irony, in an accent so unlike his own and with such an exaggerated curl of scorn on his lip, that the people in the room were left in little doubt that he was portraying an inspecting officer of the RUC addressing a squad of policemen ranged sheepishly before him as he confronted them with the unmistakable evidence of their laxness in apprehending law-breakers, in the form of the barracks charge-book, not as full of summonses as it ought to be.

Mr Stuart remarked shrewdly that maybe one or two of the bobbies might have put in for promotion or a transfer to a more salubrious neighbourhood.

'Oh here, right you are Tom,' said Mr McCabe with a start, as if he might otherwise have left out a bit of charade, illustrating how an inspection of the charge-book could panic the ambitious or the favour-seeking into rushing out to summons people. He cast Mr Stuart in the role of easy-going policeman and glared at him penetratingly.

'Not much from you in here, Constable Stuart,' he complained bitterly in the false middle-class accent. 'Do you not like summonsing people? Is that it? Are you making friends with everybody instead of doing your duty? Is that what it is?'

Mr McCabe resumed his normal voice and said very seriously that for an RUC man to have it asked of him if he was getting friendly with the people was as good as a black mark. That was why there would be a rush to fill up the charge-book coming up to an inspection. And what was more, he went on to explain, the easy-going ones that had maybe been shutting an eye to this, and looking the other way from that, might be the worst of the lot when the fear gripped them. The other ones, like your bold Billy Blake there, you know where you stand. It's the easy-going ones you have to watch,' said Mr McCabe sadly.

'Of course,' agreed Mr Stuart shrewdly, 'the friendly likeable bobbies would have been let see more than your Billy Blakes, and no doubt that would stand to them when the need arose and they were out looking for people to summons.'

'Oh right you are Tom,' said Mr McCabe. 'Never trust a policeman.'

Mrs McCabe and her sister protested at this sort of talk in front of the children and said disapprovingly to each other to listen to what they were drumming into the young ones.

'Pardon me,' said Mr McCabe rebukingly to the women, 'this is not hooligan stuff. This is very far from being corner-boy talk.'

Mr Stuart's uncle, who was called Old Sam, had been nodding vigorous agreement during Mr McCabe's discourse and occasionally letting out those heartfelt groans and sighs of assent favoured by religious people listening to stirring sermons and which are sounded as much on the ingoing breath as the outgoing.

'Oh boys no,' he said with a fervent groan as he drew a deep breath when Mr McCabe said never to trust policemen. Old Sam had been listening with the eagerness of one who himself had some testimony to give. Indeed, on several occasions when there had been a pause in the talk, he had said very meaningfully that he could tell them a story about the peelers so he could, oh yes, oh boys ay, and had accompanied this claim with very significant winks and nods, to say nothing of very knowing looks, all meant to induce people to ask him to tell it. In due course a pause went on long enough for him to tell it anyway, though not without once having to relieve his feelings by spitting excitedly into the fire, forgetting, so strong was the sense of the past aroused in him, that it was not his own fireside he was at, that he no longer had a fireside of his own.

'I was coming out of the signal box one night,' began Old Sam, for he had been a railwayman all his life, 'when I spotted this boy near the level crossing.'

Old Sam came from the town of Ballymena where the
word *boy* has many other shades of meaning besides the
customary one: a lively entertaining man; a shrewd
bargainer; a man of enterprise; a bold forward man; a
tricky man worth watching; a stranger about whom little
is known; in short a man of any age or character playing
any part in any episode or encounter, all depending entirely
upon what is being related and the subtle nuance of tone
of the speaker.

Even in the dark Old Sam knew that this boy at the
level crossing was a peeler from the peaked cap and the
way that he stood. What, Old Sam asked himself, was this
boy doing there, though of course he was not old then,
which, he told them, was getting on for thirty years before.

'Is it me this boy is waiting to catch,' Old Sam had
wondered, and at this point he explained about the lump
of coal. He was in fact carrying under his arm partly
tucked away beneath his coat, and in any case wrapped
in several pages of the *Belfast News Letter*, as if it were a
light package, a fine big lump of coal just the right size
for carrying home as long as you didn't have too far to
go. There was this boy, said Old Sam, who left him down
just such a lump from the engine tender every time he
passed. Great coal it was, Old Sam claimed wistfully, a
lump like the one he had with him that night having, it
would seem, the property of sitting quiet on top of a fire
all day long and then, at no more than a tap or two –
you would hardly call it poking – would make a blaze at
bedtime you could roast a bull at. And Old Sam spread
his hands wide at the fire before him but clearly conjuring
up a vision of another fireside that had been his own,
or rather that of him and his sister, a fire into which he
could have spit to his heart's content. (Such a collection
of old bachelor men and spinsters on Tom's side, Mrs
Stuart was often heard to say, that couldn't even get

themselves married like the rest of us, and God knows, she would add scathingly, you wouldn't think that was a hard thing to do.)

'Howsomever,' said Old Sam, coming back to his tale, 'what was this big boy going to do? Would he let me pass?'

Well first he said to Old Sam that it was a nice night and Old Sam agreed that it was and then he asked Old Sam if he thought the next day would bring rain but in such a way that Old Sam had to stop to answer him. When that topic was done with he sought Old Sam's views on another.

'This boy chatted and chatted,' said Old Sam, 'you could hardly name what that boy didn't chat about.'

All the time the lump of coal was biting into Old Sam's arm but he daren't shift it to the other arm to get ease and something told him he mustn't seem too impatient to be on his way. Old Sam turned over in his mind the question why that boy was in such a chatty mood and he resolved upon one thing. This boy is not sure, he told himself, if he was sure he would search me but he's not sure. And that will be the rock I'll cling to, should he chat till morning.

Old Sam uttered the phrase about the rock very triumphantly and with shining eyes as though the words were something more than a mode of expression for the decision he had come to and were literally the form – a message of guidance – in which his course of action had been revealed to him. He repeated the words about clinging to the rock with great satisfaction, leaving nobody in any doubt as to their significance, and very stirred himself by the recollection of them. That was the moment he spat into the fire. He leaned forward excitedly to send a stream of saliva hurtling into the flames where it made a thudding noise against the red hot coals and sizzled on the bars. Mrs Stuart glared not at Old Sam but at her husband, who thought it politic to put on a frowning face and make mock scolding noises such as are used to display exaggerated disapproval to children – or dogs.

'Hah. Haw,' Mr Stuart growled at Old Sam, shaking his head in deprecation. But Old Sam was only put out momentarily by the reprimand. Eagerly he undid his cuff and rolled back his shirt sleeve to reveal a brown stringy forearm knotted and veinous with age. For of course he had clung steadfastly to that rock of his through the long-dragged-out minutes of polite chatting, during which he had betrayed not the slightest sign of pain in his cramped arm, which, as he now demonstrated, he could not completely straighten out after thirty years. What was more, he said, the little finger had no feeling in it.

'You could stick needles in it,' he boasted proudly and the children, who had been craning to see how his encounter with the peeler had left its mark on him for life, would have liked to have asked to see this done. They did ask, however, though from people generally rather than from Old Sam himself what would have happened if the policeman had found the coal on him. It was Mr McCabe who replied.

'Terrible times,' he said sternly. The Railway Companies, he said, were as bad, if not worse, for sacking men with years of service and then seeing to it that they got work nowhere else. He said that you daren't blot your copybook with people like that or you might starve.

As Old Sam rolled his shirt sleeve down again, still salivating with remembrance of the days of his strength and of his trial by ordeal, Mr McCabe referred angrily and scornfully to the numskulls who talked fondly of the good old days. Good old days! What was good about them was that that's when we were young, he said, and then added with a sigh that it is always good to be young.

Mr Stuart said that just the same you could get a good house then for eighteen pence a week and maybe a perch of land thrown in. Mr Stuart was famous for reciting what things cost when he was young before the Great War and of what could be had for small sums of money even in the way of lettings, rents, leases and perches of land thrown in. Sometimes he made everybody laugh when he claimed how little it cost to keep a wife then compared to now and Mr McCabe would then laugh more heartily than anybody and go on to take up Mr Stuart's theme more vehemently than anyone else, calling upon them all to marvel at having started up on his own at the shoemaking with five pounds from his father to buy a stock of leather. Five pounds! God help us all! Five pounds!

As the women made some tea and Mr Stuart busied himself around the grandfather clock with something that involved the plopping of a cork, Mr McCabe withdrew a little into himself to muse and sigh about times, which hard though they were, had nevertheless shaped him and them and made them what they all were.

A little while later Mr Stuart replenished the glasses of those who were partial, not forgetting to whisper discreetly into the ear of certain of the women that they might like a drop of this instead of tea. Then he expressed the opinion that Mr McCabe should give them a song instead of sitting there laying down the law and leading the women astray. But it was a little early for that. Mr McCabe was holding forth on the subject of marriage, about which he had a stock of much quoted savings both serious and light. These he could bring out with an impressive delivery, very solemn with the serious ones but so lively with the light sayings that he went into fits of laughter himself at them and flung himself back in the chair so boisterously that Mrs McCabe called out sharply he would have it over. It prompted them all into the recollection of famous love matches; scandals; carrying on; old bachelors once-jilted; old maids who had been beautiful; youthful folly.

Mr McCabe took a fat neighbour woman on his knee and made a pantomime of the foolishness of youth besotted by love, filled with illusions about women, their delicacy, their vulnerability, the need to protect them within the shelter of strong arms. It was this last aspect of the feelings that seemingly he and the rest of them had harboured when they were young that they now found most comical, the women as well as the men, for they all roared with laughter when he represented the ridiculous urge of youth to treat women as babies by miming, with the fat neighbour woman on his knee the action of a mother chewing food into pap and then transferring the pap from her mouth to the child's.

'Was that not it,' he demanded, choking with laughter, 'eh, what, was that not it?'

He slapped his thigh in delight at having hit it off so aptly while the women merely pretended to be shocked and said what a terrible man he was, but shrieked with merriment.

'Hey? What?' he asked suddenly, startled out of a train of thought induced by these matters when his wife called out sharply to him that Tom had asked him to sing, and then, noticing that his glass had been filled while he had been engaging in what she referred to as his old foolery, protested, 'here, hi, no, the half of that glass would do.'

But he very graciously agreed to sing and rose to his feet. He cleared his throat and raised his hand. People thought he was about to start singing. But it was first to say a word or two about the song before he sang it.

'Sir Harry Lauder sang this song,' he announced very gravely. 'This was Harry Lauder's song: "Keep right on to the end of the road".'

Mr Stuart said they wanted to hear John McCabe sing

it. Mr McCabe sighed and said that they would have to bear in mind that it was very powerful stuff. It might let him and then again it might not. You could never tell with powerful stuff like that.

'We have every confidence in you,' said Mr Stuart, 'away you go.'

Mr McCabe sang the first two verses of 'Keep right on to the end of the road' in a pleasant baritone voice, not as powerful as his speaking voice, and accompanied the words with many of those gestures and expressions, which, from pulpit and stage, are used to uplift the poor in spirit and encourage the faint of heart.

> Keep right on to the end of the road,
> Keep right on to the end.
> Tho' the way be long let your heart be strong,
> Keep right on round the bend...

As he sang he turned slowly to address each part of his audience in turn in so accomplished a manner that the fat neighbour woman whispered an enquiry to Mrs McCabe had he been on the stage and then whispered her amazement at being told tartly that he had not.

But at the third verse he faltered and was unable to go on. He drew a handkerchief and blew his nose while the people smiled nervously and waited. Mr Stuart watched him over his glasses. Mr McCabe cleared his throat and everybody thought he was going to resume singing. But he had something more to tell them about the song.

'Sir Harry Lauder was on the stage singing this song,' he told them very solemnly, 'when it was whispered in his ear that the only son had been killed in France.

'What did he do?' Mr McCabe asked them all rhetorically. 'What did he do?'

Mr McCabe paused before he informed them.

'Harry Lauder turned to face the audience. He finished the song.'

So too did Mr McCabe in a voice, which, weak and quavering at first, grew steadily stronger.

> Where all you love you've been dreaming of
> Will be there, at the end of the road.

He prolonged the last phrase as long as he possibly could in a most triumphant manner with arms outstretched, quite heedless of his wife's admonition to watch out or he would clear the lot from the mantelpiece with that sleeve of his.

Mr Stuart led the applause as he made for the grandfather clock and opened a little door in its stomach from which he produced a bottle quite openly. Mrs McCabe said it was time the children were in bed and reluctantly they did as they were bid.

'There you are,' said Mr McCabe, 'there you are.'

He gazed round upon them all with a beaming smile, accepting congratulations not only, it seemed, for singing the song, but also for having in the course of it, surmounted a great obstacle, for having been able to carry on at that third verse where the terrible news from France had been broken to Harry Lauder. When he sat down smiling as the children trooped out of the room, his eyes were wet with tears.

Upstairs the children lay for a while listening drowsily to the muffled voices coming up from below. It was then that the little McCabe boy remembered the smell that had engulfed him when Constable Blake had bent down over him to take his cap gun. The smell had been made up not only of rubber and sweat but of something else that he would not have been able to tell them about when he told the story. It was the same smell as when Mr Stuart plopped the cork out of the bottle from the stomach of the grandfather clock. He lay listening to the merriment below for as long as he could fend off sleep and then he dreamt of Harry Lauder performing before the Crown Heads of Europe with a lump of coal and the *Belfast News Letter* and of his father's muffled voice declaiming something about Wellington praying for night or Blücher at Waterloo.

3

The blackboard was a dark swift-flowing river that all must cross. Stepping stones were words you spelled correctly. The children all went ah-ah in pity when someone fell in. Faces turned round to stare hostilely at Joe McCabe when, at the very first, he had gone ah-ah along with the rest, not knowing that, as an Infant, he was not supposed to be able to read already, which however was the case, and he had stood wretched at the railings, ashamed for being different, gazing sick for home towards his father's shoemaking shop where he had made ships out of old wooden lasts and hammered lace-holes into them for port holes, quite content with his way of life.

It had been intended that he should go to the new school on the Dublin Road rather than the small old school on Chapel Hill near Mr McCabe's shop. The Chapel Hill school must have dated from the first Education Acts of Parliament for it had no other name than 'The Free School' except for a nickname 'The Raggedy', deriving from some distant association with the early ragged schools for the poor. The headmistress had claimed Joe as soon as she heard of him and had informed Mr McCabe of her decision in tones which settled the matter once and for all. When Mr McCabe spoke of this he always thrust out his chest to convey the idea of a large woman with a bosom and a regal bearing and he imitated a woman's high voice, but imperious and severe: 'I'll take him. He'll be perfectly all right with me.'

Every morning a tiny Austin car deposited Miss Pym

at the gate. After she had strode majestically into the school some of the bigger boys, of whom Joe was for a time secretly terrified, would re-enact her arrival in the small car. By means of engine noises made with their mouths and expressive leaning gestures with their shoulders they depicted the tiny vehicle as labouring up Chapel Hill with a heavy list and then springily righting itself as soon as it was relieved of its monstrous burden. But there was something in the way the charade was done that made it less a caricature of Miss Pym than a tribute to her eminence and power.

The nickname 'The Raggedy' was much resented by the pupils of 'The Free', and Joe was always apprehensive in case he might have to fight when it was called out at him disparagingly in the streets through which he had to pass, for he was more timid than he dared to show. Once there was a pitched battle on the Boiling Well Meadow at the mill, between boys from the Free School and boys from the big new school on the Dublin Road which had a clock with a square tower on it, grounds with flowers and vast playing fields. Joe ran when the others ran, both on the rushes forward and on the tactical retreats, crying out 'The Free, The Free' as a battle-cry amid volleys of stones, and he was astonished and delighted to learn that he was deemed to have played an honourable part in the battle. It was from then that he stopped pining at the railings for home and his father's workshop.

Joe got into trouble with his mother for letting out that he sometimes swapped his lunch with a child from one of the poor houses up an entry near the mill, claiming that what was between the other child's bread was far nicer than his own. His mother was shocked. Swapping his good lunch that thousands would be glad of for God knows what! Nicer than his own indeed! His mother and his aunts pulled faces of disgust at the idea of eating anything from that quarter. There was ringworm up the entries. There was nits up the entries. There were dirty heads. Did he want to bring her home a dirty head? Was that what he wanted? As if she didn't have enough! That poor child, she told him sternly, is being reared on condensed milk and margarine. The condensed milk tin, she explained to him, sits in the middle of the table till it's empty. Then, she instructed him, they either rip open another one, or, she added, exasperated at his ignorance, they go without.

Being able to read already, he soon moved out of the Infants. He was put in a class where they did adding tables by first chanting them to learn them by heart. To this Joe responded by first going rigid with bewilderment and incomprehension and then, in the middle of a flood of tears at the teacher's desk, suddenly seeing how they worked, so that everything was all right and he did not even have to do what some of the others did in their sums, which was to silently go through the tables moving their lips and beating time with a finger.

There were pictures of the months round the walls. In each of the pictures a handsome girl and boy did things appropriate to the month. In January they built a snowman. In April they walked smiling in their raincoats through a shower of lightly slanting rain. They had fun in all the months. They looked as if they would have had a job to tell which month they had most fun in. In some of the months the handsome parents looked on smiling at the lovely children having fun. The boy and the girl were so beautiful that Joe was in love with them both and sometimes when he lay in bed at night he would think of them kissing him passionately.

He was proud of being sent out to Jenny Black's to buy a cane for the teacher. There were two Black sisters and the children never knew which was Jenny. They were old English ladies deposited there by God knows what receding tide, and they pronounced canes as 'kines', just as, when Joe went in on his own behalf to ask about toy wooden aeroplanes, they bent down over him wonderingly and repeated 'aeroplines?'. Their little shop was full of cheap toys made in Japan and cheap delph of the kind that the people drank their tea from in all the poorer houses. Joe heard his mother and his aunts speak of the mothers of children not as spoilt as they were slipping out to Jenny Black's on Christmas Eve for some wee cheap thing to put into a child's stocking. They kept a large stock of canes to cater for all tastes and Joe would be asked by them very sweetly – for they were unfailingly courteous – the name of the teacher the cane was for so that they could carefully select one to suit, whether thin and whip-like or thick and bruising like a club. Proudly would he bear the cane back up Chapel Hill with the change clasped firmly in his other fist, anxious to be seen fulfilling the important trust that he was honoured with.

When the women at their doors saw him pass by with the cane held importantly high they would remark to each other on its significance. Their remarks were amused and approving.

Would learn nothing without it!

Oh hammer it into them!

Not do them a button of harm!

Never did *us* a button of harm!

The virtues of physical chastisement at school were upheld on all sides, even by mothers like Joe's who almost never beat their children themselves. A stern regime at school was felt to be necessary not only scholastically but for general well-being. All sorts of infantile disorders were thought to be cured by it. Thumb sucking. Nail biting. Stuttering.

Spare the road and spoil the child!

Couldn't watch them!

As soon as your back is turned!

Oh hammer it out of them!

I told mine the day he started if he come home crying he had got a slap I would give him another one for good measure.

There were people in the neighbourhood of whom it was said with a laugh and a shake of the head that the cane had never been out of Miss Pym's hand during their schooldays, that Jenny Black's thickest canes had made no impression on them.

Somebody will feel the weight of Miss Pym's arm behind that cane before they are much older, said the women at the doors fondly as Joe went by. Most of the caning at The Free School was attributed to Miss Pym even though, as Joe was to find out, some far more painful cuts were administered by teachers paler in character and less memorable. It was simply that Miss Pym dramatised her punishments in a manner that was awesome to behold.

The first time Joe saw this was in the playground. A rumour circulated among them during play break that there was a boy smoking in the lavatories at the end of the playground. Even as Joe was trying to take in the enormity of such daring and wickedness there was a sudden quiet in the playground. Miss Pym strode through them, cutting a swathe of awed silence as she moved. She had her yellow cane in her hand and she went straight into the boys' lavatories. The children waited excitedly for what would happen next. Did the sudden silence in the playground first alarm and then strike terror into the culprit as he waved frantically to disperse the thin blue smoke, so aromatic, so wicked? What would his feelings be as Miss Pym's terrifying figure suddenly filled up the door of the cubicle and touched him lightly with the yellow cane, ever so lightly, not at that stage to inflict pain, but merely to shepherd and marshall him out of his sinful den, out past the reeking oozing urinal, out into the sunlight in front of the waiting children, excited and expectant? When Joe was older he would learn that our perceptions at such times are strangely heightened and that we become exceptionally aware of small things, of the surfaces and textures of things, of scuff marks on shoes, loose threads, shapes of passing clouds, or perhaps, in this case, of feeling, amidst Miss Pym's angry denunciations the faint patter of her saliva falling like light rain upon his neck.

The malefactor was a big lump of a lad and Miss Pym spent a little time arranging him into a suitable posture to cane his open palms, pushing and pulling him this way and that. The pushing and pulling made it seem almost as if a struggle was taking place, as if the wicked lump of a lad was resisting her, even wrestling with her... But it was a struggle in which the outcome was never in doubt and the cane whistled down upon his open palms, gripped at the wrists. The awesomeness of the spectacle was in no way diminished by Miss Pym's rage and spluttering denunciations, far from it. Long after Joe had forgotten the sight of the actual blows and the subsequent blubbering and cursing of the boy hugging his red and throbbing palms, he remembered with awe the sudden manifestation, the great rage, the ferocious struggle, the inevitable victory, the sure and certain retribution for wrongdoing.

On the rare occasions when a mother would complain about a child being beaten the protest would lose any significance by reason of her being a well-known quarrelsome woman, notorious for having loud and foul-mouthed public rows with everybody: neighbours, relations, husband, publicans, the police. Sometimes such a woman would be heard shouting abuse in the corridors and once Joe's teacher slammed the door of the classroom and stood against it, agitated and trembling, till the shouting died away. The woman was the mother of the Connor children and it was because of them that Miss Pym again made one of her dramatic appearances before Joe's class.

It was a grey cold winter morning of the kind when those near the fire were envied. Joe had already got into trouble for the way he had answered the door to the gypsies before setting out for school. A gypsy woman with a ragged child had thrust an artificial flower into his hand, saying eagerly, 'only threepence the dozen, sir, ah sir,' enlisting him as an ally with the absurd flattering 'sir, ah sir' and the sight of the small dirty child, so that he had taken in the flower hoping his mother would buy. 'Tell them not to-day thank you,' his mother told him, showing him the little false smile he was to use to accompany these words but he had been unable to do it so that she had snatched the flower from him and got rid of the gypsy woman and her child with far harsher words, as if to show him what he might have spared them. On the way to school the gypsies were going from door to door with their gaudy flowers and at one door a girl who answered it gave a simple shake of her head and he thought sadly that yes, that would have been kinder. Behind the girl he caught a glimpse of a glowing fire and an old woman sitting at it in a shawl. He thought enviously how nice it would be to be that old woman and not have to go to school on cold mornings.

In school the Connors arrived very late and, strangely, were not reprimanded for it. The Connors were often late and the teacher was usually angry; once they were caned. But this time it was very different. The class could tell that something odd was happening concerning the Connors and that the morning was not going to follow its usual routine. First the people near the fire were moved so that the Connors could sit there instead. The little boy's teeth were chattering. Other teachers came and looked at them and conferred in low voices. Then Miss Pym arrived. She first looked sternly at the Connors and then strode out again purposefully. Was it her cane she was going for? Were the Connors going to be caned by Miss Pym? Was it for being late? Was it ringworm? Was it the police? But when Miss Pym returned she was carrying a little parcel which was ripped open quite angrily to reveal – her lunch. They knew it was her lunch because she ate just such a lunch every day in her large classroom with the oilskin maps on the walls, reading the *Belfast News Letter* as she ate. Once when Joe was sent on an errand for her she got him to read a passage from the *Belfast News Letter,* eating the fine white sandwiches as she listened and mingling with her comments and corrections the occasional particle of chewed bread. Oh it was Miss Pym's lunch all right, and she made the Connors eat it, standing over them almost angrily till they ate it all up, every pick.

At break a rumour swept through the playground that Cruelty was in the school, that the man from Cruelty was with Miss Pym, though some of the children maintained that Cruelty was a woman and arguments broke out over this point and became noisy. The Connor children were standing by themselves at the wall, the little boy clinging to his sister's hand. Suddenly the playground went quiet as the people looked up and saw Miss Pym at an upstairs window watching them. The quiet spread across the playground like the shadow of a cloud on a bright day. Then they noticed a figure behind Miss Pym, but vague and indistinct. Was that Cruelty, they speculated excitedly? Eagerly they strained to catch a glimpse of Cruelty. Then the window went blank and the children broke out chattering, telling each other that Cruelty was coming, that Cruelty was going to appear among them, right in the playground!

But it was Miss Pym alone who appeared. She strode across the playground to where the Connors were and led them into the school, one in each hand. They were never seen again.

A little later Joe again heard the name of Cruelty spoken in the school. It was in the corridor. Two older girls were quarrelling loudly. The one who seemed to be getting the worst of it suddenly rounded on her more strident adversary and reduced her to confusion and shame with a reference to Cruelty, bitter and wounding.

'One thing sure,' she cried triumphantly, her voice ringing off the walls of the corridor, high and proud, 'one thing sure. Cruelty never crossed *our* door.' And added very cuttingly, '*my dear.*'

But it was after he had moved upstairs into the older classes that Miss Pym was sent for on an occasion of direct significance to Joe. Their readers that year were proper books, stiff and hard-backed. When the two piles of readers were laid out on the teacher's desk, the one of old used readers for those who could not pay and the other of brand new ones for those who could, Joe's was one of the first hands to shoot up to show that he had his money ready. He loved the new school books. He loved the springiness of the still unbroken spines, the bright colours of the hard backs – which, alas, he would only have a day to admire before his mother's thriftiness made him cloak them in brown paper. He loved the smell of the newly printed pages. Above all he loved that smell. Time and again he would press his face against the pages just to inhale their fragrance.

He loved the stories in the new hard-backed reader. The icy Snow Queen who rode the north wind for a chariot. The Gorgon Medusa with snakes on her head for hair who could turn you to stone if you as much as looked at her. He was impatient when the teacher stopped the readings to explain the meanings of difficult words for he would have preferred to infer much richer meanings from the text around them. Valhalla. Pomegranates. Widow's weeds. The widow's weeds occurred in a story about King Henry. The story must have come from a bigger story for it ended without telling you the ending, whether the widow's petition was granted by the King. On the page opposite was a picture of King Henry, a burly middle-aged man with his hands on his hips. Perhaps he looked like that when the poor widow was finally let in to see him after being kept waiting for days. The teacher explained to them what widow's weeds were. Black from head to toe. Not a stitch on her that wasn't black. But who has died and why is she so poor if she had once played with the King when they were children and he was a handsome little prince? What does she want from the King? Is it money? As she sits waiting she thanks God that the young ones are safe. But safe from what? Are they rebels? Are her menfolk in the Tower? What is the reference to a scaffold? Is it a pardon she is after? The story in Joe's reader ended just as the door of the King's chamber swung open to admit her to his presence and there was the picture of the King confronting you with his hands on his hips and a cold hard face. Long after they passed on to other stories Joe would leaf back to the picture of King Henry, wondering how the King could not grant her petition for the sake of old times and the happy games on the grass at Richmond. Time and again Joe studied that hard face for some inkling of a happy outcome.

They had nearly finished the stories in the reader when one day the people near the fire were moved so that Joe could sit there instead. Miss Pym came and looked at him and conferred softly with the teacher and he did not remember very clearly being taken to his father's shop across the street, nor whether he was carried home, nor how long he lay in bed before the doctor's huge cold rough hands felt his stomach, nor whether it was night or day when the doctor carried him out into the cold air and there was the smell of petrol that he used to like so much, hanging round cars and lorries to get a whiff, and then the sweetish suffocating smell of ether under lights and he plunged down into a whirling redness of pain and thirst in which every atom of his being concentrated upon sucking at the drops of water on the spout of a white cup that was sometimes put to his lips for a moment or two and then cruelly torn away again.

He got used to overhearing visitors in the ward point him out as that handsome little boy in the bed at the window who had been very ill but had now quite definitely turned the corner. Although still weak he was entering the convalescent stage and was beginning to appreciate and even to enjoy the attention which his grave illness had earned him. He expected from visitors, in addition to solicitude and presents, a degree of awe at the nearness he had been to death. He listened complacently to his mother when she related to visitors the episodes that dramatised this, as for instance when a band of little girls from his school had stood below on the street gazing up at the windows of the hospital on one of the days after the operation when his life had hung in the balance. Sometimes he prompted her if she left out something which particularly highlighted the consternation he had caused or the esteem in which he was held.

One of the nurses had been especially good to him, a rosy-cheeked young woman from the country. She had even given up her time off to sit by him constantly when the slightest thing might still have killed him. It was she who had tended him all the terrible night long when he had screamed incessantly for water. She had wet his lips from time to time with the spout of a drinking cup. He had fought her when she took the spout away, for he had burned with thirst. With unremitting patience she had time and again let him have only just enough to ease his torment.

But all that was in the past. Now he was the pet of the ward. Even the patients, or at least the longer-staying ones, shared a little in the achievement of having pulled him through. Some of the nurses could not keep from kissing him occasionally. And not only the nurses. There was a youth in the ward with some vague ailment, the older brother of one of his school-mates, who also kissed him, and full on the mouth too, which he did not like, but did not know if he ought to express that dislike openly. One of the nurses was beautiful. She was tall and pale. She did not make a fuss of him like the others did but sailed by, very cool and grave, oblivious of his wide-eyed admiration. On days when there were no visitors and he had been made dreamy with reading books, the sight of the tall beautiful nurse roused in him longings which it would have shocked him to associate with her directly; instead he would bring to mind the image of one of the little girls who had gazed up at the windows, and in a languid reverie would dream of clasping her to him through the long drowsy hospital afternoon.

Although he could now eat certain solid foods, everything he ate was supposed to be first submitted to the inspection of the Sister. As time went by some of the nurses began to be a bit lax about this, though not the stout country girl who had nursed him so devotedly and with whom he was now very familiar, cheeky even, especially when visitors were present and he was anxious to show off to them how privileged was his position and the liberties he could take with the nurses.

But the nurses who were a little indulgent about letting him eat some of the nice things that were brought by visitors had to be careful not to let the chief Sister catch them departing from her strict orders. She was a plump older woman, very short of breath, and at first sight the very picture of motherliness, but in fact she was a stern disciplinarian, more feared than the matron and notorious for dealing out harsh reprimands in the most contemptuous and wounding manner in front of everybody: patients, doctors, visitors even.

One morning the affectionate youth took advantage of there being nobody in the vicinity of the boy's bed to be more demonstrative than usual. The youth addressed the boy in the same manner and with the same terms of endearment that the women used when they made a fuss of him: darling; pet; love. The youth gave the boy a long lingering kiss full on his mouth which disgusted him. He rubbed his mouth with his knuckles in disgust and anger. He struggled away and began to whimper. The youth in alarm set about placating him and finally succeeded. He brought him a large chocolate biscuit to seal the matter.

Some of the chocolate biscuit was still lying on his locker when the fat Sister waddled up breathlessly to change his dressing and her eagle eye spotted it at once.

'Who gave you that?' she asked him sharply and when he made no reply she called out to the nurses hurrying about the ward, 'Which one of you let this patient eat a biscuit?'

When that too brought no answer she ordered them to stop what they were doing and attend to her. They gathered round his bed. The tall beautiful one was there and so was the country girl with the ruddy complexion.

'Now,' she asked him again, 'which one of them was it?'

His bedclothes had been drawn back to reveal the

stitching which now closed an enormous wound that had been kept open for weeks to let a system of tubes and bottles drain away the poison of a burst appendicitis. He was quite used to being displayed to groups round his bed and indeed had come to enjoy the awe which the sight sometimes inspired that his delicate body could have survived such a catastrophe. But this was a very different kind of attention he was now attracting. The manner of the Sister, coupled with her bulk, was so like that of the headmistress at his school when she loomed terrifyingly over people to get to the bottom of something that it produced the same feelings of fright and the same impulse to blurt out anything that would bring the awful interrogation to an end. This was not the kind of attention he had got used to in hospital, far from it. This was not being marvelled at and admired, spoilt and cuddled. He wanted nothing whatsoever to do with this kind of attention. He just wanted it to go away and for things to be as they were before. He would have to blurt out something.

'It was her,' he said, pointing at the stout nurse from the country and filled with relief to get it over and done with so that things could get back to what they were before.

The nurse was so shocked and disbelieving that for a moment or two she hardly protested her innocence but merely looked from the little boy to the Sister in dismay. The Sister spoke the nurse's name in a very ominous tone which they all recognised as the prelude to administering one of those public dressing-downs for which she had a reputation and in which – amongst the upbraiding and castigation – she added the personal disparagement which made it so wounding.

Had she not given the strictest instructions? Did a young nurse like her think she knew better? The Matron would hear of this! She should have stayed looking after farm animals! That patient had been at death's door. Was she too ignorant to know that? It wasn't beasts round the farm she was tending here!

The poor nurse burst into tears and fled from the ward. The rest of them dispersed, the tall beautiful nurse disdainful of the whole business.

The boy did not at first understand the guilt and self-reproach which attacked him. He was not sure what it was exactly he blamed himself for. It had happened so suddenly. He had had no time. It had blown up in a moment and then was all over.

But why *her* a voice asked him, why *her* of all people?

What answer could he give? That he had pointed in panic at the nearest face? But that was only partly true. The nearest face had been that of the beautiful nurse. Even in the moment of panic he had been acutely conscious of her looks. Wasn't that the reason he had not pointed at her? And did not this apply in diminishing degree to all the other nurses ranged around him until he arrived at the nurse with the plainest face and therefore the one that mattered least?

The chilling thought came to him that he had been – quite suddenly and without warning – tried and found wanting.

The thought disturbed him for a while, though it was not remorse it prompted but resentment. He felt unfairly used. He felt that his own handsome face had been used as an instrument – completely against his will – by which there showed itself the cruel face of the world, and, until he put it from his mind, he lay quiet and sullen with resentment.

4

They loved playing forts that year. Sounding the last post. Uttering the names of places like the Khyber Pass. They liked holding out in forts just as much as surrounding them. One of them had an air gun. There was a hut on the Boiling Well Meadow with a tin roof. How they made the air gun pellets ping and whine off that tin roof! It was hard to tell which they enjoyed more – being besieged or besiegers – when those air gun pellets sang through the air.

One day was particularly exciting. There were Zulu warriors involved. Sammy Jackson was a Zulu warrior with grass tied below his knees in the Zulu fashion. Sammy chanted and did war dances. Hula lula, heap big Jula. Sammy was still chanting as they trooped home, weaving in and out of them with his spear and his grass garters.

But Sammy never knew when to stop. No matter what it was: a new slogan; a new riddle; the latest catch phrase from the wireless or the pictures; Sammy kept them up long after the rest had tired of them. It was the same with being a Zulu warrior. They had all enjoyed themselves. But it was over. It was done with. They now looked forward to their tea, to reading their comics round the fire: the *Hotspur*, the *Rover*, the *Wizard*, the *Champion*. They wanted to be quiet with their thoughts in the aftermath of exhilarating play on a mist laden autumn afternoon, one of those afternoons when the onset of darkness is infinitely gradual and there seemed always to be just enough light left to play for just a little while more. Joe loved the autumn. He sometimes thought that autumn was the true time of vigorous awakening after the languor of summer. They were no longer in the mood for Sammy's interminable Zulu war dance. Joe wanted to be alone so that he could listen to a voice in his brain reciting the poem 'Hohenlinden', full of banners and bravery, that was in the school poetry book.

> On Linden, when the sun was low,
> All bloodless lay the untrodden snow,
> And dark as winter was the flow
> Of Iser, rolling rapidly.

But Sammy Jackson kept on gyrating round them, prancing and chanting. Hula lula, heap big Jula. So somebody shot him with the air gun and then dropped it. Somebody pointed it at Sammy's backside and pulled the trigger. They had to take him to the infirmary to get the pellet out.

There were repercussions in school the next day. Who had done it? Who was the one? Why should they all be blamed because of one? Miss Pym lined them up against the map of the world and made them all stand there while she conferred on the landing with Mr Jackson. Then she spoke very gravely about Borstal and Approved Schools. But contrary to the general expectation she did not use the cane on them. Miss Pym saw that it would have done no good. She had no firm suspicion which one of them it was. Miss Pym never beat confessions out of people unless she knew them to be guilty.

Mr Jackson took it very badly that the truth was not beaten out of them. Mr Jackson was a small man but very fierce. He was nearly old enough to be Sammy's grandfather. He had been a horse trooper in the Boer War and had bandy legs, though not, some said, from the horses. He complained to the neighbours with great feeling that if it had been the other way round he would have got it out of Sammy all right. Mr Jackson firmly believed in not sparing the rod. He took off his belt and showed it to the people he spoke to. If it had been the other way round, he assured people bitterly, there wouldn't have been an inch of Sammy he wouldn't have left a mark on. He thought poorly of neighbours who wouldn't show him the same consideration.

Then the war came and one of Sammy's brothers was killed in action. Mrs Jackson came out onto the street waving the official telegram and crying her son's name. Her married daughters joined her wailing and lamenting. She went from door to door crying his name. The streets seemed filled with bands of wailing women and gaping children.

The Jacksons were a military family. Two other Jackson boys were in the forces as well as sons-in-law. They were very loyalist. Their walls and mantelpieces were bedecked with patriotic mementoes in all their forms: pictures of royalty, Orange Order regalia, Coronation and Jubilee mugs, photographs of numerous soldiers and sailors. When the victory at El Alamein was announced and the church bells were rung for the first time since the war to celebrate, that was not enough for the Jacksons. They organised their own celebrations in the tin-roofed hut sometimes used for Gospel Mission Campaigns. They started the Alamein celebration quite early in the day. From the windows of The Free School the Jackson daughters were seen escorting their mother from door to door, got up in a dress made entirely from Union Jacks, she making rueful deprecating gestures occasionally as if to show that it was the daughters' idea not hers, but smiling just the same. They came into the school, meaning to exhibit her in all the classrooms, but Joe saw them only for a brief

moment or two on the landing framed in the classroom
doorway. Miss Pym stood beside them for a few seconds
while the fifth and sixth classes looked at their flag thus
patriotically embodied. Then Miss Pym flashed her smile
upon it and upon the class, that powerful smile of hers,
brilliant but chilling, with which she could bring all sorts
of things to an end. Joe saw the women again from the
window, still going from door to door but giggling
sheepishly.

The party in the Gospel hut was more successful. Joe
had only ever been in the hut on religious occasions,
for sometimes there were Gospel film shows about
missionaries in hot countries, and these, being free of
charge, always drew a number of boys, hopeful, as they
clutched the Gospel hymn books up at the front under
the stern eye of the preacher, of seeing heathen savages
with spears or perhaps wild animals on the badly flickering
screen, in between the fervent praying and the lusty hymn
singing.

> I am coming Lord,
> Coming now to thee.
> Wash me, cleanse me in the blood
> That flowed on Calvary.

For Joe the party was memorable for two things. The
first was that Sammy Jackson showed them how to
masturbate at the back of the hut. He wiped away the
pearl-coloured drop containing the seed of life and said
that he could give a girl a baby now.

The other thing was that Mr Jackson was taken ill at
the top table where the drink was and he was brought
down among the boys at the lemonade end. One of his
married daughters brought Mr Jackson to Joe's table.

'Tell the boys about the kopees,' she said encouragingly

to give him something to lift his mind. The kopees were
in Africa, she explained to the boys to start him off.

From what they could make out of what Mr Jackson
said in a passionate voice a little the worse for drink, the
kopees were some kind of hills in South Africa where
great battles had been fought with the Boers. But the
boys did not listen very attentively. They did not care
much about the Boer War. Indeed they despised the Boer
War. It was used as a term of disparagement. When they
saw pictures of ramshackle articles of war belonging to
inferior nations they would label them contemptuously
Boer War. That's a Boer War battleship, they would sneer,
that's a Boer War aeroplane. The term, for some mysterious
reason, stood in their minds for anything military that
was obsolete, second-rate, not quite the real thing. Even
Sammy with one brother in the roll of honour and two
others serving in what was undeniably a real war could
afford to look rueful when his father spoke so passionately
of the kopees of Africa.

Not long after Alamein Sammy Jackson officiated with
great authority at the killing of his father's horse for the
pig-meal factory. Nobody quite knew why Mr Jackson had
acquired the horse which he kept in an abandoned builder's
plot near his house. Perhaps it reminded him of his time
as a horse-trooper in the Boer War. Children gathered to
see if he would ride it but he only led it about the field
and slapped it soothingly with his hand; when he was
gone they made fun of his bandy legs. He did not come
to the field when the horse was killed. Sammy took charge.
He suddenly seemed to grow older after the incident with
the air gun. He never again played at Zulu warriors. He
went around with youths, worked for money at all sorts
of things after school. Sometimes when Joe reflected on
it long afterwards it seemed almost as if Sammy Jackson's
childhood had been brought to an end by a single shot.

45

Like Sarajevo. At the killing of his father's horse he held its head and made gruff soothing noises. He told Joe and the others to keep back, to keep well back there. After the man shot the horse and it fell in a heap Sammy helped to winch it up onto the lorry. The horse's soft flabby lips fell open in a terrible smile.

5

The Battle of Britain had been at its height when one of his aunts died. She was buried from his grandmother's house. People in the crowded house of mourning told each other the latest count on the news of the numbers of planes shot down. Eighty of theirs, twenty of ours. They spoke these numbers uncertainly as if testing each other's understanding whether they were good or bad. The children were taken up to see their dead aunt laid out on the white bed in the big front bedroom filled with flowers and their sad fragrance. One of the men gathered round the bed spoke; first of their aunt in a low but matter-of-fact voice when he said *so she got away then*, then in much graver tones, *eighty of theirs, twenty of ours.*

One of Joe's older cousins had a model German bomber and they were allowed to look at it so long as they kept quiet. No playing, they were told. It was a Stuka dive bomber and was beautifully painted with swastikas and black crosses. Joe said eagerly that he knew why the wings were bent into their odd shape. He was eager to impress. It was to facilitate coming out of the dive, he said, but to his dismay his cousin repeated scornfully *facilitate! facilitate!* where do you get these big words from? He told everybody that Joe had swallowed a dictionary.

They were allowed to ride back from the cemetery in one of the black coaches drawn by a black horse. They liked that part of funerals. They liked the gentle motion, the houses gliding silently by the windows, the soft clip-clop of the horses' hooves. His older cousin who had made the Stuka dive bomber pushed Joe down on the leather seat and held him helpless, then he coolly, deliberately, spat upon his mouth. He let his spittle gather like a flower of white foam upon his own lips before spitting it onto Joe's. Joe was enraged but pinioned and impotent. The others were uneasy at what he was doing to Joe and said to let him go which he did with a shrug, saying casually it was nothing, at his school people did that all the time.

One of their dead aunt's daughters, Vera, was almost exactly Joe's age. Vera and Joe were always quarrelling and making up. Vera loved dressing up and doing turns. She could draw a Fu Manchu moustache round her mouth, put her hand up her sleeves, and be a Chinkee Chinaman. After her mother died Joe was told not to fight with her as much in case it made her cry for her dead mother. He was always ashamed when she cried and would do something to make it up to her. He took her to the pictures to see *The Wizard of Oz* where he fell in love with Judy Garland and it was only later he realized how like Judy Garland Vera was with her big dark eyes, her song and dance turns, her grace. It was a wet Saturday afternoon when he took her to *The Wizard of Oz*. There was such a crush at the 6d Pit Entrance to get in out of the rain that Sticky Sloan, the doorman from the main entrance, came round to keep order. He had a raincoat on over his puce-coloured uniform with the scarlet epaulettes and he was wearing bicycle clips. Vera and Joe had been told not to tell their grandmother that they went to the pictures, for their grandmother was an Elimite and did not believe in the pictures. Their grandmother had a canary that could come to the bars of its cage and pick you a little scroll of paper from a box of them where they were packed like a honeycomb and when you took it from its beak and unrolled it there would be a text from the

Gospels: 'I am the way, the truth, and the life' or 'For where your treasure is, there will your heart be also'.

Vera sang Judy Garland's song 'Over The Rainbow' at the concerts which she and some other girls put on in the shed at the back of their grandmother's. She lived at their grandmother's after her mother died. At the concerts Vera also did all the announcements and there was lemonade made from fizzy powders which they got from the shop that sold Vera's film star magazines. Vera was a keen student of the private lives of the film stars as revealed by the film magazines, their marriages and romances. If the name of a glamorous film star was put to her she would confidentially disclose some intimate and slightly shocking fact about them in the same tone with which their aunts gossiped over cups of tea in the kitchen: eager, soft but scandalised.

When Vera was asked to choose herself a kitten from a litter, she did so unaware that she was passing sentence of death upon the others. She called her kitten Bimby and tied a blue bow round its neck. She was not supposed to see the other kittens put to death and the aunts were angry at Old Sam for drowning them in front of her. Vera was horrified. Old Sam sat on a stool beside a bucket of water placidly smoking his pipe and drowning the kittens one by one, letting the rest play round his feet, laying out in a neat row their bedraggled little bodies so different in death to what they had been in life. As they drowned they clawed upwards towards the light. For long afterwards Vera would hug Bimby to her in his blue bow and murmur endearments in a tone of indignation at what might have been his fate. Vera and Joe had seen the kittens being born though without realising at the time that that was what they were seeing. It had been in the kitchen while the women talked and Vera noticed that the cat was behaving strangely, the one-eyed cat that kept you on its good side. Oh look, Vera and Joe said, the cat must have ate some black thread, for there's a black thread coming out of it. One of the aunts had done something rather strange. She had said poor pussy, and carried it out very tenderly. The way she said poor pussy gave Joe a little shock of embarrassment. He sensed that the way she said it was something very private to do with women, that only women would say poor pussy like that.

The shed where Vera and her cronies gave their concerts had tin sides which magnified the sound of anything striking it. On one occasion when they were doing song and dance turns devised by Vera there was a loud drumming and rattling noise. It was Old Sam pissing against the corrugated tin wall. Vera was furious and the aunts were not pleased either. The uncle got into trouble for making light of it. He looked at Vera over his glasses and asked her if people did not do things like that where she came from, which was the Shankill Road. Vera reported to Joe with satisfaction that Old Sam was in trouble with the aunts for stealing their church peppermints and hoarding them in a drawer in his room. She lowered her voice to disclose confidentially that the aunts had also ruled that anybody could sit in Old Sam's chair as it wasn't his at all.

Old Sam's chair had lions' heads carved on the arms and the feet were paws. It was under a picture of Daniel in the Lions' Den so that for a long time the children thought that chair and picture were connected. It was also beside the radio and Old Sam listened to the war news intently, though to nothing else. News about the Russian Front excited him and he was proud for always maintaining in the darkest days that the German eagle would never beat the Russian bear. Old Sam would hurry past the window where the aunts sewed, looking at his silver watch and they would say dear bless us is that the time already as he made for his armchair by the radio and put on his glasses to listen to the war news. The Russian General Timoshenko had caught his imagination and at the mention of his name he would thump the lions' heads in excitement. That fella, he said triumphantly, is an ordinary working man that put himself through night school. Long years afterwards when Joe saw in the papers that Marshall Timoshenko had been given a state funeral in Moscow it was of Old Sam he thought and the lions and Vera and Bimby in his blue bow.

Vera took Bimby with her when she went back to the Shankill after the bombing of Belfast. People wondered with an amused half-sigh how long Bimby would last on the Shankill in his blue bow. Just before she left she and Joe quarrelled over the house-training of Bimby. Vera said that Joe was cruel to Bimby and cried. Joe was so sorry that he offered to set his model boat on fire as a spectacle to make it up to her.

His model was of the *Great Eastern*. He had read about it in a *Book of Ships* that he loved to read, lying on the sofa in his grandmother's kitchen while the aunts baked bread or ironed or gossiped. He read it more than once and he had favourite chapters. He never went straight to the chapters that he liked best but made himself read preceding ones to save up the pleasure. He liked the chapter headings. 'Oar and Galley'. 'The Wooden Walls of Old England'. 'The Iron Clads'. 'Paddle Wheel and Screw'. But most of all he liked the account of the *Great Eastern* and the sonorous name of the man who built it, Isambard Kingdom Brunel. He made a model of it from the pictures in the book, though he liked lying on the sofa dreaming of it better than doing it. He loved lying on the sofa half-dreaming, half-reading amid the smell of baking bread and hot irons. He would fall into a reverie over a picture of the *Great Eastern*, cut away to show all its places: on the deck men in top hats promenaded with ladies of the utmost respectability while down below in the engine room the bearded engineers, as grave as statesmen, sternly oiled the massive pistons. When Vera cried because he was cruel to Bimby he said he would burn the *Great Eastern*. He thought he would do that not only as a means of restoring himself to her grace but also to re-enact the real happening when the *Great Eastern* caught fire on her maiden voyage. He would wet it with methylated spirit and set it alight realistically on the Lagan Canal nearby. He found out where the methylated spirit was among the objects that he liked to turn over in the old shed that he heard them say had been a weaving shed once. He smelt the methylated spirit and tasted it for he had heard the aunts talk in whispers about it. It was when he had been lying on the sofa with the *Book of Ships* half-listening to them say softly but ruefully that it wasn't always easy to tell when the uncle was on the bottle and that when he was it didn't do to keep him too short of money because – and here their voices were lowered so much he caught only the words 'primus stove' and 'methylated spirits' before he was asked sharply what he was doing blinding himself with that small print so close to his eyes on such a nice day when he should be out in the good fresh air. The taste was awful. How could the uncle drink such stuff, he wondered in awe.

Vera had Bimby with her when they went to the water's edge among the reeds. There, on the still surface of the Lagan Canal at dusk, the *Great Eastern* blazed with a beautiful blue flame, its feasting revellers scalded and blackened in the shambles of once gorgeous saloons.

When the car came to take Vera back to the Shankill she couldn't find Bimby. It was not long after the one o'clock news on the radio and somebody asked where was Old Sam. Nobody knew that either. Vera put the two absences together and wailed that Old Sam was drowning Bimby. The uncle was sent to hunt for Old Sam to prove to Vera that he was not, while everybody else looked for Bimby. In the middle of the confusion Old Sam appeared holding a little box. The box had holes neatly drilled all around it and at the holes was the occasional glimpse of Bimby's glistening little black nose. Vera looked out of the car as it drove off and held up the box for Bimby also to say good-bye as he headed for the Shankill in his blue bow.

Vera was delicate and once when she was recovering from an illness she came again to stay at their grandmother's. It was before she left for the country. They said she would do better in the country. She was in the big front bedroom that Joe would always associate with funerals. Even though it was a bright room with big windows he could hardly remember seeing a living person in its large bed, only the dead.

Joe sat so long at Vera's bedside that the light faded and an aunt suddenly came in, suspicious of what they were up to in the dark, but she found them simply murmuring together quietly. Yet the aunt's suspicions had not been entirely unjust because when he heard that Vera was back again at their grandmother's he remembered with a flutter of excitement how she and he had played together, and of the form their play had sometimes taken after they had quarrelled and were making up.

There was a flower that grew in a brass pot near the landing window at their grandmother's. It had bell-shaped flowers and if the bell was squeezed a golden drop appeared which tasted sweet and which Joe said was honey. He had told Vera about the drops of golden honey one day when they were not speaking but were looking for an excuse to break the silence. Eagerly she had watched him squeeze a drop onto his hand and then she licked it off and he did the same to hers. But most of all he remembered that once they had been very naughty together, that he had been too scared to do more than look, except just a little with his finger and then only very timidly. When he went to see her with film star books and magazines it had undoubtedly crossed his mind that he might remind her of that, and then ... perhaps.

But the time slipped by with them only murmuring together. He watched with fascination how Vera seemed to grow more beautiful as the shadows deepened. Her large dark eyes and her little nostrils and her lips seemed to blossom into a softly luminous mask of perfect proportions. Why, he wondered in astonishment, had he never discovered her beauty until then?

She died later that year.

He was taken in to the room filled with flowers to see her laid out. But he came away bearing no lasting impression. As time went by the image faded and was entirely overlaid by that earlier one from that evening at their grandmother's when he had watched Vera's face shine with beauty for a little while in the fading light, when, fascinated, he had watched her beauty and bright eagerness dissolve and fade away in the darkening room.

6

It was a bright autumn day. The children sitting at the windows of the upper classrooms of The Free School watched covertly the never-ending convoys of army lorries carefully thread their way through the anti-tank barriers on the street below. The anti-tank barriers posed no obstacle whatsoever to Patsy Boyd's pig cart which swerved through them with style, Patsy addressing the pony with stern commands as he stood upright with the reins like a charioteer, a favoured boy riding proudly on the tail behind the swill bins, but a council steam roller was brought to a halt hissing and palpitating, then, thwarted in its purpose, it retreated backwards down the hill, furiously whirling its machinery.

All morning the piece of paper with the verse written on it in block capitals had circulated among the boys of the sixth class and at break time they discussed it eagerly. It was objected by some that there was no such word as 'manufacts', but if the whole word 'manufactures' was put in it spoilt the rhythm of the line; it would not sound right. Then Joe had an idea. Put in the word 'fabricates'; that would do it. It meant the same thing. But the others were doubtful. Some had never heard of the word and scoffed. Those who had heard of it thought it too brainy. Joe is far too brainy, they complained. But Joe challenged them quite hotly to try it and then proceeded to demonstrate how well his word fitted by earnestly reciting the verse with it in. 'Long and thin goes too far in/ And does not please the ladies/ Short and thick just does the trick/

And *fabricates* the babies.' He was quite breathless when he had finished and flushed with embarrassment at having recited poetry in the playground. But they were not won over. They stuck to 'manufacts' as on the slip of paper. They felt they had no right to go changing something they were only to pass on.

Who has it now, someone asked and a girl's name was mentioned. They all looked a bit shocked, though mostly in wonderment and awe at the idea of girls reading a naughty thing like that. The girl was one of the English evacuees who had arrived when the war started. She was from London and was very pretty. Her frightened air and twittering London speech were very appealing so that some of the boys had a tendency to become rowdy and boisterous in her presence and inflict crude brutalities upon each other which it gave them pleasure for her to see and to shrink from. She had a sweet coaxing voice and large dark eyes that she could open pleadingly. When they had a singing lesson Joe fancied it was her flute-like voice he heard above the rest with its strange exciting note of reproach and appeal. Her name was often chalked in those love circles in which it is stated baldly as a fact that so-and-so loves so-and-so.

They had singing after break. First they sang the 'Road to the Isles'. It was not a song they liked. This was not just because of the fast sequence of Scottish place names – Lochranoch and Lochaber and so on – that most of them could not pronounce as quickly as the lively song demanded, but also because the teacher scolded them to adopt a cheerful vigorous singing manner for which she set them an example at the piano which appalled them by its false heartiness. They preferred slow sad songs like 'Shenandoah'; 'Ye Banks and Braes of Bonny Doon'; 'Drink to me only with thine eyes'. Then the teacher got the pretty evacuee to sing 'Ye Banks and Braes of Bonny Doon' all by herself.

Her voice rose and fell as expressionless as a flute. She sang it without any expression but earnestness and it seemed to make the song even sadder and more beautiful.

> Ye banks and braes o'bonie Doon,
> How can ye bloom sae fresh and fair;
> How can ye chant, ye little birds,
> And I sae weary, fu' o' care!

It made Joe want to do brave and heroic things in her sight, like when she had appeared one evening where they were playing round the anti-aircraft gun on the Boiling Well Meadow. He had swarmed up a beech tree that he was usually timid of climbing, hoping that the others would remark loudly on the smoothness of the bark of beech trees making them dangerous to climb, and so perhaps impress upon her some notion of adventurous daring, though as he had climbed into the high canopy the activity below had moved away, leaving him higher than he should have been, alone, and suddenly afraid.

It was geography next. Miss Pym the headmistress took them for geography. The big oilskin maps were unfurled behind Miss Pym's table. Miss Pym read out important facts about the places she named and located them with a long yellow pointer. Sometimes she got one of the class to use the pointer, usually one of the clever or attentive pupils, but now and then one of the other sort, as a kind of test they were doomed to fall, and so they could be made an example of, could be denounced and derided, could have their faces pushed against the shiny surface of the map with the faint tarry smell that never left it, could finally have the yellow pointer wrested from them in disgust and awarded like a prize to the more deserving.

Joe was very good at pointing. Not for him the shame of letting the pointer wander off and get hopelessly lost in the oceans and continents or the closely congested cities of the industrial centres of civilisation. He loved the vivid colours of the different countries of the world: the bright blue of the seas and oceans; the red of the British Empire; the darkening shades of brown as the plains and valleys gave way to highlands and the mountains rose to peaks. He followed coastlines unerringly. He traversed great mountain ranges that divided continents in two. He rounded the Capes on which the great sea-lanes converged from every port and then fanned out again to go their separate ways. Joe loved geography. He thought how wonderful it must be to have come back from those exotic places full of tales, travel-stained, indelibly marked by it, pointed out for it, set apart because of it, *bearing the aura* of it in the local streets and parlours – else what would be the point! His Great Uncle William had been round Cape Horn and in the South Sea Islands, but Joe did not think that counted since it had conferred no *aura* upon him. Old Uncle William lay all day long in his bed with his white beard and called out to Joe and the others when they passed his door to tell him whose were the visitors' voices that he heard below. 'Who's up the hoose,' he begged to know, and they hurried past his door without telling him and sometimes they heard him questioning Uncle Tom without avail when his sheets were changed and he was made to sit on the edge of the bed with his thin pale legs the colour of lard and never a sign that he had been in the Islands of the South Seas or round Cape Horn. No, that would never do for Joe!

Joe stood tirelessly before the great map of the world and fulfilled his role with pride until the map of the British Isles was hung over it and Lena Wilson took his place. For a little while longer Miss Pym continued to read from the geography book. But the time came when she felt that the class might be getting tired of the facts and figures about the places which Lena pointed out quite faultlessly, for she too was a good pointer.

The attention of the class appeared to be wandering. At the mention of the dull word 'manufactures', so dry and abstract, there was even rustling and whispering which Miss Pym attributed to boredom. In any case Miss Pym herself was apt to get drowsy from too much reading aloud without the opportunity to declaim and dramatise which so enlivened her reading of poetry – as in the poem celebrating the chivalry of General Stonewall Jackson in the American Civil War: 'Who touches a hair of yon grey head/ Dies like a dog! March on! he said' which Miss Pym always recited in a high chant.

So she turned instead to telling them about one of the many Cook's tours she had been on before the war, and Lena traced out its course on the map of England. The class liked it when Miss Pym did that. They liked to hear the small incidental personal details which she would casually let drop as she described famous places or celebrated views. A packed lunch that day. Lost a hat over the side. The guide rattled it all off pat. Got a glassful each to try on the way out. Fit for nothing that night but bed. Everybody on a donkey, a boy at its head.

When the tour Miss Pym was describing reached Portsmouth, Lena proudly held the pointer to the place in which Miss Pym and her party had stood on the very spot where Lord Nelson had died on the *Victory* at Trafalgar.

Lena flushed with pleasure when Miss Pym gave her a little nod of praise for being so good with the pointer and this almost made Joe jealous until he remembered how he had steered the pointer through mazes of rivers and deltas to find cities with ancient and sonorous names that were bound to strike a chord of romance in all who heard them. On top of that he liked Lena. They all did. She was gentle but strong and protective. She helped to settle quarrels and came to the rescue of weaker ones being bullied. She had even come to Joe's rescue only the day before. He was being teased by a group of older girls some of whom would soon be leaving school to work in one or other of the mills whose tall chimneys were all around like tall red towers, though it must be said that the girls saw their going out into the grown-up world as a liberation and were restless and excited at the prospect. Two of them had begun to make a habit of pulling at Joe and tickling him and of taking liberties with him which he disliked and which would have been absolutely out of the question with the older boys. Lena had told them off quite sharply. For goodness sake, she had said, catch yourselves on; away and have some sense! and they had let go of him immediately.

Miss Pym suddenly pounced on a girl at a desk at the aisle and wrenched triumphantly from the girl's hand the slip of paper with the wicked verse on it. It was when they were taking leave of Admiral Nelson's great ship the *Victory* and some of Miss Pym's tour party had grumbled about being done out of their afternoon tea that day, which Miss Pym, clearly dissociating herself from that faction, said *hadn't pleased the ladies*. The ripple of unrest which manifested itself at these seemingly innocuous words had finally convinced her that something was going on and she had tracked down the source of it with a skill sharpened by years of practice in watching rows of pupils out of the corner of her eye and waiting for the right moment to pounce. In this case it was when the piece of paper had reached a desk to which – in spite of her bulk – she could leap in an instant.

As she read the grubby slip of paper a shocked silence fell upon the class. The girl she had found it on sat white-faced and trembling. Everybody was paralysed at the enormity of the fact of Miss Pym being confronted with things with which she could have no relation, which belonged to another world entirely. They wished fervently that they could go back to the time before Miss Pym had read the verse. They squirmed under the burden of knowing that Miss Pym now *knew*. Time seemed to stand still in the classroom even though they could hear it rush on carelessly in the street outside.

'Where did this filth come from?' Miss Pym asked in a terrible voice, clicking her tongue in shocked disgust. She read it again and clicked her tongue even more.

For a moment or two the dead silence in the classroom continued. The horn of a lorry was so sharp that Joe felt it strike almost painfully on his ear. Patsy Boyd's pig cart clip-clopped into the hush of the classroom and they all heard distinctly each word of the cheerful salutations which Patsy exchanged with the people as he drove hard through the anti-tank barriers charioteer fashion.

Then Lena spoke. She was standing quietly beside the forgotten map of the British Isles.

'It was me, Miss,' she said. She was nervous but resolute. 'It was me,' she repeated.

Miss Pym was dismayed. So was Joe. He had expected Miss Pym to track it down to a very different section of the class, had supposed indeed that Miss Pym had already arraigned the prime suspects before her in her mind as a preliminary to beating it out of the culprit. But all she did to Lena was to ask her in a tone of bitter disappointment where she had got it from.

'Outside,' said Lena sadly but firmly.

Lena as she spoke indicated with the yellow pointer the windows and the street. In one of the windows there was framed a tall mill chimney streaming a white plume. It seemed to be moving on past cloud after cloud. It made them all seem in motion, it and the school and the roofs of the houses on the street; all seemed to be part of some vast ship that sailed serenely through the sky and into the great wide world.

The air-raid siren went and Miss Pym issued immediately the 'Disperse To Your Homes' instruction to those who lived nearby while she marshalled the others in the playground before leading them to the air-raid shelters.

Sid Gorman took some of the boys of the sixth class, including Joe and his friend Roy, to the back garden of the Horse Shoe Bar, otherwise known as Gorman's. There they looked about them with curiosity and excitement. They felt excited at escaping from school and also at disobeying Miss Pym's instruction, and they were curious because most of them had never before been where they now were. They had only managed to catch a glimpse of it when the gates were opened for the Guinness lorries, for it lay behind a tall hoarding covered with Guinness Is Good For You advertisements. Great barrels lay around in every posture that a barrel can be in, some full and immovable, others empty and lolling idly against each other. They thought how wonderful it would be to play games among the barrels, games in which silence and concealment would alternate with the clamour of discovery. But they did not like to suggest this for they had to take their cue from Sid who was a squat strong boy quite capable of forcibly expelling people who did things in the yard that got him into trouble, and then of picking on them in the playground for a long time afterwards. In any case Sid did not play that kind of childish game. He was much too serious. When he went into the house for a drink of water he came out looking very grave from what he had just heard on the wireless.

'The Russians are still holding out around Minsk,' he announced solemnly.

The others did not reply. They did not even exchange looks. Only when Sid was safely out of sight would they take the risk of mocking his precocious adult mannerisms, for he was very strong and could be brutal. They looked instead at the huge mound of corks that cascaded from a loft in the corking and bottling shed. They would have loved to have waded into that pile of corks and sent them flying. They felt strangely touched by their clean fresh look and longed to stuff their pockets with them as a prize to gloat over in solitude.

'We are going to have a battle,' Sid announced. Did that mean pelting each other with the corks, they wondered hopefully.

It did not. It meant bombing the American Pacific Fleet in Pearl Harbor. Pearl Harbor was on a patch of waste ground just beyond the jumble of barrels. Solemnly Sid led them to it. There the American Pacific Fleet lay in formation, line upon line. It was made up of dozens of model ships, or rather representations of ships. A ship consisted of a flat piece of wood with a structure of corks. Cork gun turrets swivelled realistically and the guns were nails. Roy enquired about several that had no guns and everything was on one side. Aircraft carriers, explained Sid tersely. One of the other boys found a small parcel of nails, some of which were red with rust. Sid appropriated them immediately, saying he had lost them. They are six-point-nine-inch guns, he pronounced, used on effing cruisers of the J-class. Sid was famous both for his cursing and for his frequently aired knowledge of the technicalities of the ships and aircraft and tanks that figured so prominently in the news: JU–87 dive bombers; pocket battleship Scharnhörst; Panzer division; 20-millimetre cannon; Marshal Timoshenko; four-point-five-inch gun turrets; Admiral Yamamoto. On the wall near the bottling machine was a large map of Russia with red and black arrows pinned to it, ugly and grim, not like Miss Pym's maps with their bright colours, shining with history and adventure.

'The bombers are over there,' said Sid, 'on the Japanese fleet.'

They did not like to say that all they could see were several very crude looking representations of aeroplanes, also made from corks and scraps of wood; these lay on the ground each with a neat pile of stones beside it. Where was the Japanese fleet?

'The planes have already taken off from the carriers,' said Sid coldly. 'They are approaching Pearl Harbor.'

He spread out his arms and made a noise like an aeroplane. He made other movements too, some of which they could not make out though they recognised it when he slid back the cowling of his cockpit and let his arm trail down helplessly; it was the last action of a mortally wounded pilot and it was from a film they had seen a few nights previously in the local cinema. Then a stream of Japanese-sounding orders came from his lips. He picked up one of the aircraft and told them all to do the same. His plane swooped low over the flagship of the American Pacific Fleet in Pearl Harbor and he knocked off one of its towers with a stone.

So that was what they were to do! Eagerly they joined in, vying with one another in destructiveness. Gun turrets were demolished, funnels sent flying, the air was filled with the sounds that all boys can make with their mouths to suggest the revving of engines and the boom and bark of guns. The patient work of many a long hour of Sid's in the bottling and corking shed was destroyed in a few minutes of exhilarating frenzy.

Their cries and shouts brought Ghurky Nelson the barman to the back door in his white apron with Mrs Gorman looking over his shoulder. She smiled and went away but Ghurky called out to Sid what about the bugle, did he not want the bugle? He disappeared for a moment or two then came back holding Sid's Church Lads' Brigade bugle. Several men from the bar were with him including two American GIs, all holding tall black pints in their hands.

All the boys stopped in embarrassment except Sid who kept up the bombing until there was little left of the armada of proud ships. Ghurky told the American soldiers that it was Pearl Harbor. He handed Sid the bugle. Sid became quiet and still, standing rigidly to attention. He stood in absolute silence for so long that his audience grew restless and one of the men with the pints of stout said something about the horse race on the wireless. Then Sid brought the bugle smartly to his lips and blew a long, sad, hoarse blast on it. The man who was worried about missing the horses was heard to wonder uneasily if bugling was against the law after the sirens sounded. But Sid blew on. He sounded the last post. The bugle pointed defiantly into the sky out of which the bombs had hurtled down without warning. Ghurky Nelson looked triumphantly round the group at the back door as if to get them to concede that it had been worth interrupting their horses and their drinking for. The GIs applauded loudly. The boys hoped they would hand out packets of chewing gum but they went back into the bar disappointingly.

What would they do now? Anything else would seem tame and insipid after that wonderful orgy of destruction. Had anybody any cigarettes or butts? Why didn't Sid get some off the Yanks, they complained. He said he would later. Anna gets them, he said, referring to his older sister. Joe secretly admired Anna – she was so beautiful but he was tongue-tied in her presence. Once she had come into the air-raid shelter where they were smoking and she had gently removed an American cigarette from his lips to take a few puffs herself before putting it back in his mouth again. Ah, she had said appreciatively, a Lucky Strike, my favourite. The bold film-star sophistication of the gesture and the moistness of the place where her lips had been had lingered long in his mind and he now thought with wonder and jealousy of the implications of Sid's words *Anna gets them*. The boys told each other the names of all the brands of American cigarettes. Camel. Lucky Strike. Chesterfield. Marlborough. Pall Mall. One of them produced a large bent cigarette butt and said they could all have a draw on it but it had a brown stain on the end which put them off. Look at that wet mouth on it, they said disgustedly, why do you always put such an effing wet mouth on them?

The recent sight of the GIs who had watched Pearl Harbor prompted Joe to claim that he had seen two French letters on the way to school. In actual fact he had not, common though such objects were in the alleys and lanes of the neighbourhood since the arrival of the American soldiers earlier in the year. What had happened was that he had overheard his mother and his aunt say in a scandalised whisper that some of the children, God help them, had been seen trying to blow them up for balloons, and he had wondered in amazement who such stupid children could be. But he avoided mentioning his mother and his aunt because of the difficulty of associating such things with older people other than in ribaldry.

They began playing such a ribald game now. It consisted of linking together the names of men and women whom it was impossible – and for that paradoxical reason hilarious – to imagine joined in the act of copulation. Sid at first took no part in this game, in which the name of Miss Pym kept recurring with a succession of partners drawn from all walks of life, including the church, who all had in common no more than the single feature that none of them was young or handsome. Sid was still filled with thoughts of war. He brooded sombrely over the map of the Russian Front and said again that the Russians were still holding out at encircled Minsk. He said this in very solemn tones, and the ideas which it aroused affected him deeply. He marched up and down the yard imitating with his mouth the sounds of military bands playing stirring marches, his Church Lads' Brigade bugle held rigidly at his side. Only when he had taken his fill of feelings inspired by the imagined glory of directing the great events that were deciding the fate of the world did he at last sit down with the others. He heard the name of Canon Mitchell and he enquired the reason for the explosion of mirth which it provoked. Miss Pym and Canon Mitchell, they gasped, incoherent with laughter at the absurdity of such a union.

'Yes, well,' Sid conceded with a smile but contesting the absurdity of it, 'mind you the Canon's wife had a baby only last year so he's still poking the fire.'

Sid's words instantly sobered the others and made them uneasy. The coarse adult expression shocked them for they had not meant what they had been laughing at so uproariously to have any real connection with people of their parents' generation. Joe in particular was reluctant to relate older people's babies to the same scheme of things as the girls they saw lying with soldiers on grassy banks, the French letters they picked up on the ends of sticks, the dirty jokes that were common currency in the playground and the streets.

'No,' he contradicted Sid shortly, 'he's not. He's not poking the fire. *They* don't.'

By *they* he meant not only Canon Mitchell but most people beyond the age of about thirty – and even quite young people who were plain or ill-favoured, and the others took this meaning instantly.

'How do you think they do it then?' asked Sid scornfully.

'In their sleep,' Joe said vehemently. 'They do it in their sleep.'

It was the first time he had put into words the obvious solution to a problem that had perplexed him for some time. It merely needed the right occasion for it to come tumbling out of him, expressed with conviction. He did not need to expound the theory. The others knew perfectly well that what he meant was that nature had provided for it to happen in that way between people about whom it would otherwise be quite incredible.

Sid exchanged meaningful looks with the others and smiled.

'Yes, yes,' he said indulgently with mock agreement, and tried to convey that the others were to do the same, that they were all to make an exaggerated display of letting Joe keep his childish innocence a little while longer. Yes, yes, they do it in their sleep, he repeated ironically round the group, trying to whip up a policy of ridicule against Joe.

But the others were not as sure as Sid that there was nothing in what Joe said. It reflected something that in varying degrees was still unresolved in their minds. Roy was inclined to come out in open support of the idea. Sid was outraged. They all began arguing fiercely. The controversy grew so vociferous that Mrs Gorman appeared in the yard. Her grey hair was done in a bun and she wore rimless glasses. She looked so like a teacher or some person in a position of authority that the way she addressed Sid came as a shock.

'You flaming shite,' she said coldly to him. They had heard their fathers say that Mrs Gorman had a mouth on her like a trooper. They listed in awe as she threatened to put her toe up Sid's arse. But even as she was speaking the siren sounded the all clear.

'You're not coming here again,' said Sid angrily to Joe. 'You're barred from now on.'

To make his displeasure clear he announced very pointedly to the others only that there would be another Pearl Harbor in about three weeks. Then he formed them into a file and marched them back towards the school, humming loudly the tune of a march that was often played at the end of the programme in the cinema as they came blinking and exalted out into the street.

Roy and Joe were at the tail end of the file.

'I won't come,' said Roy loyally, meaning Pearl Harbor.

The two fell further behind. Joe's spirits were raised. He hated being singled out, even by Sid. An effing cruiser of the J-class, Joe recalled, suddenly contemptuous of those cork and nail flotillas. Roy laughed appreciatively and said even more portentously in imitation of Sid's pompous manner: the Russians are still holding out around Minsk. Joe and Roy clutched each other in merriment. Roy said it was a wonder Sid hadn't said *effing* Minsk. Abso-effing-lutely, they agreed, recalling, when they could get a breath to remind each other, that Sid had even inserted his effing and blinding into a recounted conversation he claimed to have had with Canon Mitchell at a Sunday morning parade of the Church Lads' Brigade. What at the time had merely bored them with its mindless monotony now suddenly caused them to collapse in a heap on the pavement at the idea of Canon Mitchell in his flowing white robes solemnly congratulating Sid on the smartness of his platoon in language as foul as Sid's but spoken unctuously.

'Are you coming round tonight?' Roy asked when he had recovered.

'Yes,' said Joe, not mentioning that his mother had forbidden it. Joe was adept at evading his mother's questions when he went out in the evenings. He looked forward to going round to Roy's house where they could smoke or play cards and games or just sit at the fire talking, with no adults present to put limits on what they could talk about.

Roy's father was dead. He had been a driver in the Air Force. He had crashed into the back of a coal lorry on the Newtownards Road just after Dunkirk, which he had come through. He had a military funeral though no shots were fired because of the war. They were all let off school to go to it. The airmen at the graveside simply pointed their rifles up at the sky. Roy's little brother Jim cried a lot about his dead father. No matter what it was that started him crying he would go on from that to cry for his dead father.

Joe liked going round to Roy's house when the evenings were dark, as they were now. Roy's mother went out nearly every evening and the children just sat round the fire smoking, playing cards or games, or listening to Cissie Coulter from down the street tell stories of ghosts and visitations and mysterious signs and portents. Cissie was a little older than they were and her mother went out with Roy's mother in their best clothes.

Joe's mother did not like him going to Roy's house. It was because of the American soldiers. Joe had heard his mother and his aunts whisper to each other in scandalised tones that there had been jeeps parked in the street all night. Her and Mrs Coulter. But in the evenings there was only Cissie and Roy and little Jim there. They played battleships. The first thing they did was to rule the paper into squares and secretly put their ships in for the others to try to sink by calling out the number of a square.

That evening Joe got there before Roy's mother had gone. There was a jeep at the door. Little Jim had started to cry about his dead father. A big American sergeant was trying to play with him and had given him a large packet of Wrigley's chewing gum, but the other GIs in the jeep outside were honking the horn impatiently. Cissie urged Jim's mother not to worry about him crying, that Jim would be all right with her. Cissie had two little protruding teeth that sometimes gleamed in the light. She was very wise and motherly.

'You go on out Mavis,' she said to Roy's mother. 'You and Ma go on about your business. I'll soon get Jim pacified.'

When Cissie had got little Jim quietened with a mixture of endearments and sharp words they turned off the main light and played pontoon for a while for matchsticks. Then they played battleships. They played very quietly and seriously with no quarrelling or cheating, which was what made it so enjoyable. Then they turned off the other light as well and sat snug in the red firelight to listen to Cissie tell them ghost stories. Little Jim was nearly asleep, or so drowsy that he would not hear enough to frighten him. Cissie protested that they had heard all her ghost stories by now, but it was not the story itself that mattered so much as the speculation it would arouse and this was always different. In any case they could stare thoughtfully into the fire for long periods, just being cosy in the warm shadows. So she told them again about Lady Stannus and one of her visitations. Most of these were said to have occurred on the golf course which had been part of the Stannus estate at one time long before they were born, but on this occasion a mysterious woman had uttered a warning to a man who was about to pitch head first into a hole that the council had left unlighted.

Joe said that he had seen a woman near that place the day before at dark and had nearly jumped out of his skin. Roy asked eagerly if it was Lady Stannus, but Joe had to tell him no. He had gone there to smoke an American cigarette which Sid Gorman had given him in the lavatories at the end of the playground. It was dusk when he went to the Dummy's Lane to smoke it and he imagined himself to be alone. But when he struck a match a voice said almost in his ear, 'Say, give us a light, Bud,' and there, not two feet away, was an American soldier with a long unlighted cigar between his teeth. He was so startled that his hand shook as he held the match to the GI's cigar. The soldier seemed merely to be lying against the bank propped up on his elbows and at first he was aware of nothing more than his own embarrassment at being accosted while having a secret smoke and of hoping that the soldier would not tease him about being too young. Suddenly a woman's face seemed to materialise under the lighted match and he saw that she was lying under the soldier with his cape wrapped round them both so that only their heads and feet stuck out, and the woman's feet were on the outside of the soldier's. It was wonderful the way her face had formed slowly in the light of the match and whose face it was. It was that of a youngish woman who often called to see his mother about knitting. His mother and her would talk very earnestly about patterns and needles and cable-stitch and purling. She turned her face sharply to one side so as not to look at him. Her forehead glistened with sweat.

Joe tried to convey to Cissie and Roy the awe which he had felt at the sight of the woman's flushed face emanating ghost-like in the matchlight.

'Perhaps,' suggested Roy, 'it was Lady Stannus. *Pretending* to be that woman.'

Roy was very impressionable and always entered fully into the mood evoked by Cissie's stories round the fire. But not even he could suggest what Lady Stannus could have meant by such an appearance, what she could have been signalling, or to whom.

'Had the council dug a hole?' asked Roy but without much hope.

Cissie would have none of it. She pooh-poohed any notion that there was the slightest mystery in Joe's story. Huh, she said, making it clear that what he had seen was nothing other than what it had seemed. Roy and Joe began to snigger at what the American had been doing but Cissie tartly put a stop to that kind of talk for she was very strict about not allowing them to talk dirty. If they wanted to refer to *that* sort of business they had to be serious. Men, she told them were always trying to 'get round' girls. Huh, she would say darkly, they wouldn't get round *her* so easy. It was something to do with this resolution not to be 'got round' that caused her always to refuse American cigarettes. No thank you, she would say firmly, I prefer Woodbine; this in case the sight of an American cigarette on her lips would be construed to mean that she had been 'got round'. When Roy again tried to snigger about the woman Joe had seen under the soldier she got very angry. Little Jim woke up and threatened to cry.

'You'll make that child cry about his father,' Cissie warned, 'and then I'll have my hands full pacifying him.'

The mention of his father chastened Roy. Indeed it would not have taken much to make him too cry about their dead father. He said he was not a bit frightened of ghosts for his father was a ghost. Cissie gently extracted some of the packet of chewing gum from little Jim's sleep-loosened hands and gave it to Roy to share out between him and Joe. Then she carefully put a cushion under the head of the sleepy little boy to let him doze off.

'You better say that rhyme I told you about,' she whispered to Roy for having spoken that way about his father. It was a rhyme she had told them about when they were discussing places that were haunted, places that belonged to the spirits and must never be harmed or disparaged knowingly, otherwise you would have bad luck, your luck would never be good. Could the bad luck be taken off, they had asked her solemnly, feeling swept by an impulse of pity towards people who might suffer all their lives for a moment of foolishness. Well maybe, Cissie had conceded reluctantly. There were people with the gift of being able to help. There was a woman her mother knew who could make up charms and cures from secret recipes. There were things to recite. Tell us one, they begged her eagerly. She said there was one that people had recited in the air raids the year before. Some people sung hymns in the air-raid shelters, said Roy. Huh, said Cissie, that wouldn't do them much good. The people she was talking about had better than hymns. They had come through safe and sound with the street down round them in ruins. Gravely she recited the charmed words.

> This aye night, this aye night,
> Every night and all,
> From fire and fleet and candle light,
> May God preserve our souls.

Now they recited it softly again, and when they had done Joe asked Cissie where it had come from. But Cissie could only hint that it was better not to ask. It had been handed down, she said.

Indeed it had. Years later Joe learnt that it came from the time of the Vikings and the fear that they inspired on all the coasts of Europe and not only on the coasts but even far inland. Cissie verse was a prayer to be spared from an attack by the wild raiders from the sea. People sat quiet in their houses with no lights and prayed that the terror would pass them by.

But he did not know that then. He was simply awestruck by the force of the words even though he was not sure whether such words had power. Or perhaps it was that one line. *Fire and fleet and candle light.* It was both beautiful and terrible whether you thought of the things in it as forces to be appeased or invoked. It made them all quiet. They sat smoking and studying the shapes in the fire.

When Joe raced home through the blackout, resolutely averting his eyes from vague shapes and forms that seemed to loom up at him from every wall, the rhyme was still running in his head. From fire and fleet and candle light may God preserve our souls.

7

Though I speak with the tongues of men and of angels, and have not charity, I am become as sounding brass or a tinkling cymbal. 1st Corinthians 13 was one of the passages of scripture for which Joe won a prize at Sunday School for learning by heart. Old Miss Williamson, his Sunday School teacher, called at his house to tell his mother and father what a clever son they had. She always did that when one of her class learnt 1st Corinthians 13 word perfect, making a little ceremony of it as if it marked some significant stage in their development. Perhaps it was because of that verse: *but when I became a man, I put away childish things.* It prompted people to recall those for whom the learning by heart of 1st Corinthians 13 at old Miss Williamson's hands had been an omen of subsequent success, scholastic, in business dealing or in overcoming a family weakness – and of those for whom, ah God help them, it had not.

Joe had failed at the first attempt. He had left out the words 'these three' after 'And now abideth faith, hope, charity'; rushing on to the great definitive conclusion: 'but the greatest of these is charity'. The jewels of English prose in the Authorised or King James version of the Bible were sometimes rougher and less polished than the forms in which they had a tendency to store themselves in the memory where something might be omitted or smoothed out for the sake of euphony. Perhaps old Miss Williamson was right to insist on absolute word-perfectness, knowing that these erroneous forms might be deeply cherished for a lifetime and then be challenged, when, suddenly and dismayingly, the error confronts like a small betrayal. Joe had no difficulty whatsoever with the verse in which the meaning is least simple but that was because the words were so beautiful that they did not need to be fully understood. *For now we see through a glass, darkly; but then face to face: now I know in part; but then shall I know even as also I am known.*

For a long time he believed implicitly that the beauty of the words of the biblical passages he learnt by heart in Sunday School was an inseparable part of their holiness. It was almost by chance that he first learnt that the beautiful words were not fixed and immutable. When he went to a morning service after Sunday School someone had left a Bible on the pew rack. To help pass the time he looked in the Bible as the curate read the lessons, hoping to catch him out. When a psalm was sung he followed it in the Bible and not the Prayer Book. To his surprise the words he heard being sung from the Prayer Book seemed slightly different, as indeed they were when he looked. But surely it would only be the lesser known psalms, not the Twenty-third that they all knew by heart? He looked in the Prayer Book for the lovely Twenty-third Psalm, the words already in his head without the slightest effort of recollection. *The Lord is my shepherd; I shall not want ... he leadeth me beside the still waters ...* To his consternation the Prayer Book words were ... 'Shall I lack nothing ... beside the waters of comfort...'

At home they were exasperatingly indifferent about his discovery, saying yes, it always had been, everybody knew that, they couldn't help it if *he* had only just noticed it! They were amused when he became angry. He took the Twenty-third Psalm down from the parlour wall and held it out at them saying look! *the still waters.* The Prayer Book was wrong! But he knew that he was being foolish. He knew that by *wrong* he only meant *less beautiful.*

77

For a while they embarrassed him at family gatherings by referring to it, saying with a laugh that Joe was going to be as bitter about the texts as the Gospel crowd when that New Bible came out after the Great War and wasn't liked, all the old favourite texts changed, such a hullaballoo you would have thought the Pope was behind it, the Presbyterians would have had the pipe bands out if they could, the Scarlet Woman and the Anti-Christ was all the cry, that preacher the Dunmurry Pentecostalists had over from America the one that burnt the New Bible with a blowlamp in the pulpit every night for a week the hall packed to watch him, a wonder the Fire Brigade didn't object they were standing six deep in the aisles, the police too scared to go near it.

His mother's old uncle from Ballymena, though a Presbyterian, said that the Church of Ireland Prayer Book had most likely got the psalms from an older Bible than the King James. He said that the King James Bible had not caught on in Scotland as quick as in other parts. He told them that his great-grandmother had heard tell of people still using the one before the King James. His mother's uncle came from near Ballymena where some of the older ones still spoke with a Scotch accent and turn of phrase, saying *nicht* for night, *toon* for town and *wheen o' folk* when they meant a crowd of people.

'She called it *The Auld Bible*,' he said very slowly and reflectively, gazing out through the windows, narrowing his old eyes as if to see up over the houses, over the Antrim hills and the sea to where, at a distance of three hundred years, his Covenanter forefathers had marched into battle singing hymns against the Popish armies of the Marquis of Montrose.

Although the path that led from Sunday School to church was not long it was not without temptation. Another path led off it, going steeply downhill to the freedom of the streets. Sometimes he yielded to that temptation and roamed the silent Sunday streets when he should have been at church. The temptation would occur to him much earlier, while he was in Sunday School or even before that, and the thought that he would not go to church would so lighten his heart that it made him unusually biddable at home or well-behaved in Sunday School, earning him approval and praise.

As he turned unseen into the downhill path shielded by the high blackstone wall he would tuck his Prayer Book into his pocket and give himself up wholeheartedly to the whiling away of the time of church service.

He would have whiled it away very differently in church with all sorts of tricks and devices. When a psalm or hymn was being sung he would fasten his eyes upon the first verse and close his ears to the words as the choir and the congregation sang on and on, so that when he looked again and listened he would be agreeably surprised at how far on they had got; or if it was the kind of half-bright day when the sun went in and out behind the clouds he would count the seconds that elapsed between the fading of the stained glass window where a saint in armour trod upon a serpent, and its radiant lighting up again, making each second worth a shilling and seeing how rich he was.

He knew, on the streets, the time it took between the different places on his surreptitious wanderings; the high old building on the hill with the room jutting out into the street; the Catholic chapel with its brand new calvary of smooth slim marble figures; the little shop in the poor way of business where he once for pity's sake bought a dish of peas for a penny and ate them defiantly in the faces of his amused Sunday School classmates.

He was attracted by that jutting room. It conformed to

his idea of a secret hiding place in which you could not so much escape from people as be near them unseen. He thought how wonderful it must be to live always in such a room jutting out into the street with the people going ceaselessly round it like fish round a diving bell and you all snug and safe inside.

He had a school friend whom for a while he envied because he lived in a house the upper windows of which looked right into the school playground. What, he wondered, would it be like to be off school sick in bed with a book in that room and peeping from time to time into the clamour and menace of the playground. His friend and he had shared for a while a passion for the same books. One lunchtime his friend had taken him to his house, letting them in with a key that he wore on a string round his neck. His friend wanted to show him his latest book: *Coral Island* by R.M. Ballantyne. When they went in he had glanced wistfully at the narrow oilcloth-covered stairs that undoubtedly led to places from which the life of the playground could have been watched unseen. But his friend had led him instead to the yard and read to him from *Coral Island,* sitting on the lavatory with the book on his bare knees. He had striven hard not to show his disgust as his friend read a passage set among palm trees fringing a blue lagoon, but their friendship had cooled nonetheless without him finding out what it was like to watch secretly the drama of the playground in perfect safety.

The old house with the jutting room had a gable wall with a great advertising hoarding on it, a picture of such warmth and beauty that he never failed to uplift his eyes to it on chilly Sunday mornings. A spry old gentleman in antique dress sat musing serenely in a marvellous glow of firelight, attended by a ghostly servant emanating genie-like from a bottle at his side on an elegant polished table, everything reddened by the fire, snug and radiant: *Bushmills Whiskey The Spirit Of The Age.*

He had to be careful not to wet his shoes if he wandered along the towpath of the Lagan Canal. He went there only on dry Sunday mornings, for wetted shoes keep that tell-tale blue look even when they dry. He would dread the awful question: where did you get those feet? where were you that should have been in church?

He would have to listen carefully for the bell tolling the end of service. He would hurry to take his place among the homeward-bound worshippers. He would get his Prayer Book ready to slip out at the right moment and carry cupped meekly in his hand like a badge of attendance. He would think of the pew in which he would have sat and of the smell of the varnish when he leaned his head against the dark wood. He would think of the pink globe of proud flesh upon the neck of the man in the next pew. He would think of the lifting of the spirit he would have felt and of the relief with which he would have welcomed the closing words from the pulpit: the grace of the Lord Jesus Christ and the love of God and the fellowship of the Holy Ghost be with us all for evermore Amen.

He would think of the cool marble under his feet as he moved with the people in solemn file towards the arched door, and of the very different stone from which pulpit and font were made, not smooth like the marble but rough-textured and abrasive, capable – as it sometimes occurred to him to think as he lolled in tedium in the pew – of leaving knuckles bleeding and raw if they should be rubbed against its cruel surface, and not only knuckles but knees and shins and even – horrible to think of – chins and noses too.

He would think of the Prayer Book pressing reproachfully at his side like a lump of solid guilt. He would think of the well-practised manoeuvre with which it would appear in his hand as he slipped unnoticed among the worshippers homeward bound. He would think of the dull patch upon its shiny cover where his brow had so often rested upon it as he bowed his head over the pew rack in the Protestant attitude of prayer.

The Confirmation class was held every Friday evening in a room of the church hall. The boys were taken by the curate while the rector took the girls. The curate was young and modern. Word had gone round how modern he was as soon as he came to the church and people took sides over it. He smoked cigarettes. People had to get over their surprise at a curate lighting up when he made his parish calls. One of his parishioners thought it right to show how broadminded she was by eagerly proffering him a huge glass bowl for him to hold as an ash tray while he smoked and rushing to receive it from him when he had done. Others were uneasy and would have preferred a pipe. Some blamed it on the war.

The curate adopted a very free and easy manner in his instruction. The boys were all supposed to learn word-perfect the Question and Answer of the Catechism but he merely took them through it repeatedly and let them all answer in unison, reading the Answer from the Prayer Book.

Question. Who gave you this Name?

Answer. My Godfathers and Godmothers in my Baptism; wherein I was made a member of Christ, the child of God, and an inheritor of the kingdom of heaven.

The bright daylight outside made the boys restless. They felt that the summer evenings were being wasted. It seemed unfair to have to attend a kind of Sunday School on a weekday evening. Yet the curate's manner made it so unlike a Sunday School that they were not bored. Unlike the earnest Sunday School teachers with their stories of Jesus or the patriarchal wanderings, the curate conveyed to them a first faint notion of the beauty of ritual and ceremony.

The curate explained to them that they would each go up to the Bishop in turn and he would place a hand on their heads to confirm them as members of the Church of Ireland. He rehearsed them for the Confirmation service by playing the part of Bishop. As they knelt before him they saw how brown his fingers were from cigarettes. Don't wear hair oil, he admonished them deploringly with a man-to-man air that captivated them completely and they felt the thrill of discovering that such worldly things were a consideration in a solemn rite. It seemed to be an indication that they were on the threshold of adult life.

You are no longer children, the curate told them. The girls would wear white. They would also bake cakes for the Confirmation party afterwards in the church hall.

Question.   Which be the ten Commandments?
Answer.   The same which God spake in the twentieth Chapter of Exodus, saying, I am the Lord thy God, who brought thee out of the land of Egypt, out of the house of bondage.

When the curate spoke about the Confirmation party afterwards he warned them that he would not have any of that nonsense of the girls at one side of the room and the boys at the other.

High time you got to know each other, he said firmly. Stories circulated of the curate's previous Confirmation party at which he was reported to have organised games that made the boys and girls mingle and touch: blind man's buff; musical chairs; the Grand Old Duke of York;

vigorous pushing scrambling games that involved catching hold of people – catching hold of girls. *Kissing them.* No! Yes! No! Yes! They looked at each other in awe. Could the curate really be so modern?

The boy who sat next to him searched other parts of the Prayer Book for things he claimed had sexual meanings. Ask him, he challenged the others hotly when sometimes his claim was scoffed at, ask him, meaning that the curate was so modern he would tell. But they did not like to go that far, his smoker's fingers notwithstanding. When the curate was speaking of the girls being confirmed in white and Joe was wondering if it was true that they would get to kiss them afterwards the boy beside him was hissing excitedly in his ear that one of the prayers offered up by women after childbirth meant that the man had promised not to give her a baby just to get round her. He got to like the Friday evening classes, the way the curate treated them as men of the world, the surreptitious explorations of the Book of Common Prayer. You will be able to take Communion, the curate said. What is the other sacrament in the church?

Baptism, they replied.

And how many parts are there in a sacrament?

Two, they replied.

What are they, he asked, and they all answered loudly and confidently: 'the outward visible sign, and the inward spiritual grace'.

She was confirmed in a white dress like a bride. She knelt full of grace for the Bishop to place his hand upon her lovely head and he wondered with dismay if that was what he was to be denied. She lived near him. Her garden was overgrown and wild. Her father was not a gardener except by fits and starts. Long after the Confirmation party he watched her move with grace in her wild garden. Her father had once planted potatoes in large flat beds made by simply reversing the turf, saying confidently that there was nothing like rigs of spuds for breaking up ground that hadn't been worked. Then he did nothing more and so every year the potato flowers bloomed briefly and brilliantly among the tall grass. He had not known that the potato could be a wild flower of the field nor that she could be so lovely as she moved gracefully through the tall grass.

He thought with amazement of how boisterously they had kissed her in the curate's kissing games. How, he wondered appalled, could he have been so rough and clumsy?

> The Grand Old Duke of York,
> He had ten thousand men;
> He marched them up to the top of the hill,
> And he marched them down again.

Every summer when the wild potato put out its briefly brilliant little flowers he would remember her standing pensive and full of grace among the long golden grass of her wild garden.

8

Joe won a scholarship and became a blazered and flannelled pupil of a school which, notwithstanding its splendid coat of arms complete with sonorous Latin motto, was merely an efficient grind for passing examinations. Joe duly entered into its competitive academic routine and discovered that he could pass examinations with relative case. He sometimes toyed with the notion of working harder and becoming one of the elite of high performers. But this would have been more from vanity than from ambition, since the group in which his marks usually placed him, that is, the second rank just below the leaders, were there mostly because they worked hard, whereas he was there because he did not.

History was his favourite subject and he read widely for himself, disdaining the set books. Because he liked history it seemed intolerable that anybody should get better marks, and for a while he took all the history prizes in his form and once came first in Northern Ireland. He experienced, and might, had he persisted, have acquired a taste for, even become addicted to, the joy of winning, of coming first, of beating opponents. For a while he enjoyed that very special excitement which grips the examination candidate when the invigilator in the examination room lets them look at the paper and there, to his joy, are questions that send his pen racing across the pages in a kind of exultation at the certainty of trampling down rivals.

But it irked him to have to defend constantly his history

position against people who had no particular talent for it but merely swotted hard at it like any other subject, and that the history master should encourage these challengers without acknowledging the distinction.

There was a fellow called Nesbitt who wore a brace on his front teeth to correct them. Nesbitt's marks were always near enough the leaders to worry them and spur them on. Nesbitt would coolly adjust the wire contraption on his teeth before speaking, as others would adjust their spectacles – how, wondered Joe angrily, did he get away with that when others were persecuted for harmless little oddities that they could not help. Sometimes Nesbitt would be able to give a correct answer, which, for once, was eluding the clever ones, to their manifest chagrin: the mood of an irregular Latin verb, a root to a quadratic equation, or, in Joe's case, a battle or a treaty that he had not got quite right, to his annoyance.

Nesbitt was much used by the teachers in the business of keeping high fliers on their toes and he accepted the role with sly satisfaction. Joe feared and detested him.

'Yes, Nesbitt, *yes*,' the teachers would shout encouragingly, as, now and then, Nesbitt would be the only one to venture an answer, slyly fingering that awful wire thing in his mouth with obvious enjoyment.

'Tell them, Nesbitt, tell them,' one senior master would shout gleefully, jumping up excitedly from his chair so abruptly that there would be the noise of rending cloth as his gown, already in tatters from similar previous moments, caught and ripped; but still gripping it professorially at the armpits as it streamed behind him in rags, beaming his eternal pedagogue's delight at having it thus demonstrated to *them*, his stars, his prize-winners, that their places at the top must never be taken for granted, that the Nesbitts of life must never be underestimated, that ambitious mediocrity, energetic and persistent, was ever at their heels, ready to grind them down.

So Joe did not long contend in that sordid arena. He let them have their top marks, their prizes unchallenged by him, though whether from dismay or disdain or indolence he would have found it hard to tell.

He read Macaulay's *History of England* with a pleasure in which there was defiance since a man who saw him carry it away from the second-hand bookstalls of Smithfield said with amusement, 'Why, you silly boy, people don't read that old bore these days.' But Joe took to Macaulay at once. He was in awe at the magnificence of the language. He liked the ring of the old-fashioned words: apostate, rapine, calumny. He loved the passionate bias and taking of sides, the scorn, the derision, the denunciation of the Stuart Kings, the hailing of the Williamite usurpation as the dawn of liberty. He allowed himself to confuse Macaulay's indictment of Charles I with the words actually spoken at his trial, so rousing were they that it seemed as if they must have been delivered in a great speech. *We accuse him of breaking his coronation oath ... are told that he kept his marriage vow ... arbitrary arrest ... the suspension of liberty ... are told that he took his little son on his knee and kissed him ... torture, rapine, slaughter ... and it is urged in his defence virtues inscribed upon every tombstone in England.*

It was just before the invasion of France that Joe discovered Macaulay. There were military vehicles everywhere. An American tank was parked in his aunt's gateway and she spoke wonderingly of how the crew loved her soda bread. Gliders from Long Kesh circled round overhead, round and round, sometimes hanging motionless in the sky before swooping down and soaring up again, silent and graceful. The streets were filled with uniforms, and jeeps sped about everywhere. The man who had been amused at him buying Macaulay was wearing some kind of half-civilian uniform and spoke with an Englified accent. It was in that part of Smithfield where the bookshops are descended upon at certain times of the year by hordes of senior pupils in their school colours clutching their lists of set books. The man invited Joe into a high-class tea shop in Royal Avenue to tell him what modern youth was reading in war-time, but as Joe ate with relish the tasty scones and jam, the man spoke instead about women. Had Joe any experience? ... and seemed pleased when Joe confessed that he had none. The man had a large handsome face like Mussolini, with truculent jaws. Although not tall he had a mannerism of seeming to bend down with a little smile to catch what Joe said in the way that someone not used to children would condescend to a child to encourage it but only making it surly instead.

Did Joe know that there was nothing as dirty as a woman ... hmm? There was something in the high interrogative little murmur at the end of the man's queries, as he bent down with the little smile to catch Joe's replies, that, his massive *Il Duce* jowls notwithstanding, repelled Joe, though he listened in fascination as the man told him of the girl who did out his room where he lodged, whom he referred to as the skivvy, and who kept coming to his bed. He couldn't keep the skivvy out of his bed, he told Joe half-complainingly. He described in the minutest detail all the things that the skivvy would do to a nice-looking lad like Joe, what age did he say he was ... Hmm? ... and repeated Joe's age as if it was something wonderful he could hardly believe was true. It was the first time Joe had ever heard anyone speak earnestly of acts that he had only laughed over in dirty jokes and hence did not believe were real. When the man suddenly lifted his soft flushed Roman features and commanded Joe to wait there while he went to the toilet Joe instead picked up Macaulay and ran out. It was an old edition like a Bible with two columns of print to the page. He ran through the streets, carrying it unsullied like a chalice, and only when he was a long way from the tea shop did he calm down enough to be angry at himself for being frightened. Even so he felt a sudden affection for the dull ordinariness of the people on the bus into which he had flung himself in fear.

There was a passage in Macaulay which seemed familiar but he could not at first remember why. It was about the Siege of Derry. He thought he might have met it in a school anthology of English prose. Then he remembered. It had been in hospital when he had the operation. The little side ward he was put in just before he went home that had the old men in it. The old soldier who talked about the trenches of the Great War and shouted jokes in bad army French with the old boilerman also an old soldier who helped to give out the soup at dinner time. Voolez voo. Any complaints? Mercy boko. Horses had the same and they're not complaining! San fairy ann.

There was a radio play on one evening that the old men were anxious to listen to on the earphones. It was a play about the famous Siege of Derry in 1689. The old men repeatedly reminded each other what time the play was on. Joe was asked to swap his earphones with the old soldier's which were not so loud. The play was full of drum beats, marching feet, the roar of cannon and always in the background, sometimes faint, sometimes loud, the sound of a flute playing 'Lilliburlero'. A voice recited words which Joe had thought very moving even when he did not understand them fully. He thought he had forgotten them till he saw some of the words again in Macaulay. They came at the end of the play, at the moment the old men were waiting for. Some of the old men had not listened very attentively till the play reached that point, had even wandered about, asking now and then if they had got to it yet. When it came the old men became very quiet and solemn and sternly shushed someone who came in talking. It was when the little ship *Mountjoy* rammed the boom across the River Foyle and Derry was saved for evermore. So sacred a moment was it in the Protestant heritage that one of the old men got up from his bed to listen to it standing. There in Macaulay were the very words he had heard on the hospital earphones. *So ended this great siege, the most memorable in the annals of the British Isles … it was a contest, not between armies, but between nations … victory remained with the nation which, though inferior in number, was superior in civilisation, in capacity for self-government, and in stubbornness of resolution.* To the sound of a flute, now faint now loud, playing 'Lilliburlero'.

Mr McCabe sometimes spoke nostalgically of Dublin and said that it was time Joe saw it. Joe had in fact been taken there once but was so young that it did not count. A voice had frightened him with the words: *you'll catch it if the Dean sees you walking on the grass, young man*, while through an open window of what must have been a student's room was an up-ended bicycle with a tube hanging out among a litter of clothes, books and bottles making up what he now realized, from the admiring talk at school of ex-pupils who led wild debauched lives at university, had been a scene of rather studied student squalor.

We'll go to Dublin for a day or two, Mr McCabe said to Joe one afternoon when he came in from school. When? Now! said his father. What, this afternoon? Yes, his father said, and brought his fist down on the table. By God we will, he cried, and stood for a moment amazed at his own audacity.

In Great Victoria Street Station his father bumped into

an old acquaintance he had not seen for years, and Joe stood embarrassed while they loudly exchanged personal details with which to confirm or adjust the impression each had been left with of the course that the other's life might have been expected to take. Mr McCabe explained reflectively to Joe that this fellow here had once been a great breeder of wee terrier dogs and when the man not only claimed he still was but produced from the pocket of a voluminous overcoat a hairy little creature like a hank of wool with two bright beads in it he gave a shout of delight that something from the past should thus live on.

'Is he one of yours?' the man asked, meaning Joe, and when Mr McCabe told him it was his youngest the man said he looked a likely lad.

'He could do with a bit of cheek,' said Mr McCabe judiciously, pressing the man's elbow in a confidential manner, and before taking their leave the two of them agreed sadly that he wouldn't get far without it. A bit of cheek, they concluded unanimously, was as good as money in your pocket.

It was dark when they reached Dublin but even so, when they came out of Amiens Street Station he knew instantly and unmistakably that he was for the first time in a true city, a great city, a *world* city. Did the idea of a city have a reality independent of its actual buildings and thoroughfares, the idea that would reach, however vaguely and faintly, people who might never visit it? *World* cities. Dublin was a world city. Belfast was not. It was a Friday when they woke up in Dublin in the lodging house full of Trinity College students. Fish carts sped by in all directions. They ate nothing but fish here on a Friday, his father cried with pleasure, sniffing the odorous air, recapturing some Dublin element of his youth, delighted that Catholic Dublin still, as of yore, kept up the old customs in a world of change and decay. And at Ballsbridge

Show he observed with awe a monk in a brown habit of fine cloth wearing round his neck, to help him study the horses, glittering binoculars more impressive than his huge silver crucifix – such a spectacle of urbanity as could never be seen in Belfast. And his father bought a pipe in the famous shop of Kapp and Petersen where tobacco of every blend and hue to suit all tastes was measured out in gourds of shining bronze. And they climbed the Nelson Pillar, watched a play at the Abbey Theatre, strolled in St Stephen's Green, browsed in the bookshops along the Liffey, heard talk in the lodging house of Paris, of London, of New Orleans, of the shelling of the Four Courts, of the death of Michael Collins, of how worse a land Ireland was without him. Ah my poor dull Belfast, he thought, with only the mills and the shipyard to fall back on for fame when the world failed utterly to take note of your Protestant League and Covenant, even when signed in blood on the steps of your City Hall.

It had been a slow train to Dublin and they had the compartment to themselves after Portadown. His father sat at the window smoking his pipe and musing to himself on the boldness that had brought them there on impulse right there and then, that very evening, and lo, there they were, demonstrating, it seemed, how swiftly the life scene could be transformed by a simple bold decision. There was a period on the journey when the train was in a wide valley near the border with the mountains all around, though some way off, and it was evening. For a little while as he sat at one window and his father puffed at his pipe at the other the panorama of field and mountain changed so little that it was as if it were not the train that was in motion but that the world revolved slowly round it to a pleasing rhythm, that the encircling mountains, still luminous in the evening light, and all that lay beyond them, Dublin and all the great nations and cities, rotated gently round them at a still centre, that they were rocked and lulled at the hub of the great wheel of the world, and he was swept suddenly by a moment of pure rapture that all his life was still to come.

He lay awake in the lodging house listening enthralled to the night noises of Dublin, to the footsteps passing on the street outside, the footsteps of women. The landlady assured his father that Dublin was the worst city for that kind of thing by far. She had lived in London, she said. Have you, said his father, impressed. They come in here, she said, and sign in as man and wife. Out for a night's sport, his father said, with an understanding sigh.

The landlady, who had once been pretty and was still vivacious, looked a question at his father whether his son was old enough to hear about such matters and his father said with another regretful sigh that he was afraid he was.

I have lived in Paris, she said.

Do you tell me that, exclaimed his father in admiration, and listened with shining eyes to how bold a spirit she had been when she was young and confided to her with a sigh of the things that he had nearly done: he had nearly been in the Irish Guards, he had nearly gone to New York.

On their second evening there was present in the lodging house parlour a small well-seasoned man who they said had been a sea captain and who saw to it that a youngish silent woman beside him had her glass discreetly replenished. You will have seen the world, his father said to him enviously and the sea captain agreed that he had. As they spoke of distant cities a black student passed the open door carrying a bicycle, and it prompted the sea captain to tell them of New Orleans, and of the first time he had been there before he knew its ways. He climbed on a tram just like you would in Dublin except that the conductor came up to him and asked him *are you a nigger?*

It seemed he had got into the wrong compartment. The sea captain was still saddened by the memory after all the years. That's what he said to me, he repeated, *are you a nigger?* Terrible things in the world, they all agreed, and the landlady invited his father to have a bottle of stout at the same time as the sea captain was seeing to the wishes of his silent female companion. His father found that the landlady shared his appreciation for the sayings of Bernard Shaw and greeted with delight one that he had not heard before, and when she spoke of her hero Michael Collins and of the Civil War after the Treaty his father with great tact conveyed the respect of a reasonable Protestant for a brave and brilliant republican who might have led Ireland differently if he had lived. They called him the Laughing Boy, said the landlady, and then she spoke confidentially of the manner of his death. They say, she whispered quietly, that De Valera had a hand in the ambush. They spoke of the Die-hards, the Free-Staters, the shelling of the Four Courts.

What Free State? the sea captain asked them scornfully, what sort of free state is it that hasn't even its own money?

How has it not? they asked him.

Oh, said the sea captain, you mean the money with the pigs and the chickens on it instead of the crown?

He took from his pocket a Free State banknote and read from it slowly the words Payable To Bearer On Demand in *London*, to exclamations of astonishment from everyone in the room who all said that they had never noticed that before.

Are you a nigger? Out for a night's sport. Paris. London. New Orleans. He had never before heard conversation of such sophistication. He listened enthralled, the only shadow being the piano in the corner and the fear that his father might offer to sing. As well as the black student and the sea captain there was a fat old man with an English accent who pronounced cinema *Kinema* and had heard Lloyd George speak against the war with Kruger and the Boers. 'Lloyd George and Michael Collins,' said the landlady, 'settled the Treaty between them. The Welshman and the Laughing Boy.'

That night Mr McCabe sat on the bed half-musing to himself as he took off his boots.

'That woman is great chat,' he said reflectively but sadly, holding a boot for a long time, lost in thought.

There was something wistful in the way his father spoke these words, full of regret for hopes not realised, chances missed, desires unfulfilled, that Joe was shocked. He had a moment of anger against his father for shocking him with that sudden revelation of disappointment in his life. The anger flared up in him on behalf of his mother but it was too embarrassing to dwell on and he put it hastily from his mind, along with the alarming thought that perhaps the fulfilment of desire was not for decent kindly men – or for the timid.

'Here,' his father had asked him in the train on the way down when he was still full of the boldness of putting into effect at once the impulse to go to Dublin, 'here, tell me this. Who was that fella in the French Revolution, not Napoleon, the other fella, the one that said you could do anything with a bit of cheek and nothing without it?'

'Danton,' he had told his father. 'Danton. *De l'audace, et encore de l'audace, et toujours de l'audace.*'

9

On VE night there were street parties and bonfires. Mr McCabe returned with the dog from the Jacksons' where a committee for organising the street party was in full swing, and reported that so many people were gathered there, some drinking stout, that the dog had had to be passed out to him through a window because the hallway was so choked with the throng.

'Didn't you,' Mr McCabe addressed the dog with satisfaction, patting him so hard on the ribs he resounded like a drum, 'didn't you have to be passed over the people's heads like a parcel.'

From a platform erected round the Buy A Spitfire Fund Barometer a well known local church contralto sang 'Land Of Hope And Glory' to a restless noisy crowd that had previously kept breaking out into the ironical singing of 'Why are we waiting, Oh why are we waiting', to the tune of *Adeste Fideles.*

On the Jacksons' street a tall dark schoolgirl in her school colours revealed unexpected qualities of leadership by organising a kissing game with boys in a ring, directing firmly who were to kiss, while the parents smiled uneasily.

The speeches from the platform were not listened to. A brass band from the parade was prevailed upon to stay and play dance tunes to which couples began to dance spontaneously in the street. In the pauses during which the bandsmen stopped playing to take long pulls at bottles of Guinness a fat woman would try to work up a popular appeal for them to play Orange Protestant tunes by sallying out into the space cleared for dancing with her skirts hoisted above her knees and singing raucously 'The Sash My Father Wore', but without success.

A woman from Joe's street, not young but still good-looking, tried to get him to dance with her and only laughed merrily when he stumbled clumsily against her. Later he saw her just beyond the light of the bonfires on the Boiling Well Meadow with a Free French or a Belgian soldier on top of her and he thought with awe that it could have been him.

He squeezed into the Jacksons' parlour where all the men had bottles of stout and he listened enviously to Sammy's sailor brother and an Air Force man tell of their exploits in the War. Sammy's brother had been torpedoed on a destroyer in the Mediterranean which he referred to as *the Med*, though when one of the other men who had not been in the forces did the same Joe knew at once that it was an embarrassing *faux pas* and he shared for a moment the shame of the silent contempt with which the sailor and the Air Force man punished his civilian impertinence. The Air Force man passed round a fine German camera which he said he had found on a dead German. Sammy's brother and the Air Force man had armchairs and little tables to themselves on which were many empty bottles. The Air Force man said they had shot this young German parachutist as he landed on a field in Crete. He said sadly that the young German was such a nice looking young fellow when they turned him over. He shook his head with a sigh and the men pulled him another bottle of stout.

Old Mr Jackson also had a little table to himself under a picture of the *Titanic* but on this occasion he said nothing of his experiences in the Boer War.

When Joe went out into the street again the kissing

ring was going strong and the tall schoolgirl running it amazed him by darting her tongue between his lips.

He raced from one scene of revelry to another filled with excitement, partly by the momentousness of the occasion and partly by hope of adventure. Some of the streets were silent and deserted because the people were all elsewhere and in one of these streets a figure flew past him in fear. It was a youth with a foolish face who had sung very loudly 'Oh why are we waiting' in front of the platform on which were all the local bigwigs in the Boy Scouts, Girl Guides, WVS, Red Cross, and the Buy A Spitfire Fund waiting for the well known church contralto to start proceedings with 'Land Of Hope And Glory'. His pursuers were led by Sammy Jackson. They came clattering behind him, yelling cheerfully at the prospect of beating him up. Sammy offered Joe a place in their ranks to share in the fun but Joe declined even though he had not approved of the ironical singing of 'Why are we waiting' because he thought the occasion far too solemn and momentous. But he knew that that was not the reason they were chasing him to beat him up but purely because he had a big comical face with buck teeth. For a moment Joe was so touched by pity for his foolish horsey face that he thought angrily of running after them to fight at his side, if need be by lashing out at them with his feet and with curses. But he thought better of it and went instead to the bonfires on the Boiling Well Meadow where he saw the soldier lying with the woman who had clasped him to her so tightly in the dancing. The sight of them and also the memory of the dark schoolgirl in the kissing ring made him bitter that he was so ardent but so timid.

After a time all that remained of the bonfires that had blazed up so fiercely were red embers glowing faintly in the night.

The German prisoners-of-war had made a very good impression upon those whose business took them into the POW camp near Lisburn. Reports circulated of their order and cleanliness, of how good they were with their hands, of the beautiful toys they made out of scraps and of the carols they sang round their Christmas trees.

People said they wished our own soldiers were half as well behaved, to say nothing of the Yanks (the children, God help them, trying to blow *them things* up for balloons!) and then the Free French.

Oh very free indeed with what you had rather they kept to themselves!

Let fly against my walls like dogs would you believe!

Would lower their trousers on your very doorstep my dear!

He heard these reports with satisfaction. They seemed to vindicate his secret rebellion against mindless patriotism. In the books that he had begun to find on the second-hand bookstalls of Smithfield while browsing in history books, poetry books or even in novels, he had found exciting things to nourish his mental unrest. He relished the discovery of facts that made *right sides* and *wrong sides* in disputes and wars both seem less so. Nothing was more to his taste than a point of view out of step with what he had been led to believe, whether it was about historical events, contemporary politics, religion, Irish Republicanism, sexual morality, communism, or the total guilt of the Germans for the war. He was at that stage of youthful idealism when he thought that the minority views and unpopular ideas which he privately espoused existed for the sole purpose of allowing youth to flirt with them, and what is more, to regard the impulses that prompted these flirtations as evidence of nobility of soul.

One evening when he was out walking alone he met a column of German prisoners dressed in their overalls with coloured patches. They seemed such decent looking men that he felt alarmed in case hooligans would shout insults at them. One of them saluted him gravely. That night he sat over a sheet of paper experimenting with phrases for an essay he thought he might write against the policy of unconditional surrender that had been pursued so relentlessly against the Germans by Winston Churchill.

Then the newsreels in the cinemas showed the first films of the German death camps; the corpses piled like wood in a timber yard; the gas chambers, the terrible ovens. He heard with dismay the appalling laugh that went up here and there in the cinema when the newsreels showed, again and again, the scene in which a still living human creature with limbs like sticks and an absurd hat perched on its skull-like head sat among the corpses feebly picking vermin from a striped garment like a night shirt. He was sickened. He hated the people who laughed. He would have loved to help club them into the ground. He raged inwardly that Belfast could have spawned such human trash. He wished they would not keep showing the terrible pictures of the German death camps and he steeled himself for that mindless laugh when they showed the skeleton man picking at his shirt.

He did nothing to assist the spread of the term 'Belsen boy' into the common vocabulary. He hated it when fellows applied it cheerfully to each other in changing rooms and at the bathing place by the river. It was at the river that he was called a Belsen boy by burly lads proud of the new pubic hair that peeped, along with half a testicle, from their scanty bathing pants called ball-catchers on which there was embroidered in bold relief: *Belfast Corporation Baths*. His resentment was not only because of his body, which he knew to be far too slender, but because he could not reconcile the fact of the German death camps with the decent looking German prisoners, the toys

101

they made for children, the carols they sang round their Christmas tree, their dignified salutation to him on the road near Lisburn. Nor could he incorporate that terrible fact into his secret scheme of widespread rebellion against accepted attitudes, beliefs, traditions. That scheme had been based upon a policy of automatic sympathy for the *other side*. It was now utterly in disarray.

The world was not what he had thought. The world did not consist of its past, where everything is fixed, where you know what will happen next like in a play and you can study it at your leisure. The great adult world for which his childhood had seemed to be a preparation belonged only to his childhood. He felt bewildered and resentful, apprehensive, cheated. His childhood had been part illusion. He had a chilling sense of there being no firm base on which to stand, of things shifting and changing, of journeys that would never be completed, destinations that would never be reached.

These sombre youthful reflections of which he was secretly rather proud as being poetic and profound were sometimes also prompted by what seemed to him the alarming speed at which his old classmates from The Free School were growing up into men. There was the growing up of Sammy Jackson. After Joe left The Free School he saw Sammy only from time to time when he would be appalled at the rate of transformation from boy to man.

Joe sometimes saw him among the gamblers at the Sunday card schools on the Boiling Well Meadow, very smartly dressed. Sammy's clothes seemed a matter of concern to him. He did not squat over the cards like the other gamblers but stooped carefully so as not to take the crease out of his trousers at the knee. He flicked foreign bodies from his cuffs and brushed fluff from his lapels. Scuff marks on his shining shoes offended him. He was pursuing girls. Joe listened in awe as Sammy spoke familiarly of their mysteries, of the secrets of the married state, of the practices of husbands. Alec, he told Joe, referring to the man he worked for, *Alec takes it out when he feels it coming on and does it up Madge's belly*. When Joe related this to others they relished it gleefully as a comic anecdote of the uncouthness of rough and ignorant men. Joe did not relish it. I am still a child, he thought with dismay. Sammy spoke of his conquests without tenderness. Near where the gamblers gathered was a bank where the grass had been flattened into a nest by lovers. Sammy had had a girl there himself. What, Joe thought wonderingly, would that have been like. But its memorableness for Sammy lay, it seemed, in the fact that she had inconsiderately shed her blood upon him. A virgin, he complained to Joe, could ruin a good pair of flannels. Why, wondered Joe despairingly, did he have to wait so long? When would life open its doors to him and yet be so different to what had been revealed to Sammy, oh so different.

One day he heard that Mr Jackson had died. It was after they had moved to another part of town. Joe thought he would just walk past the house and look at the drawn blinds. But there was Sammy at the door looking out, a burly figure by now, almost a man.

Come in and see the father, he invited Joe cheerfully, and for a moment Joe wondered what he could mean. Was his father not dead? But then he realized it was the dead man Sammy meant. When Joe stepped into the hall he saw immediately through an open door the sharp pointed face of Mr Jackson lying on a white bed without a pillow.

What did Joe think of him? Sammy eagerly asked, and again Joe was taken aback. The only time he had ever come into close contact with Mr Jackson – except when he had been set down at the lemonade end of the Alamein victory party to tell them about the kopees of the Boer War – was when he had shown Joe's father the buckle of his belt and spoke of leaving its mark on Sammy. Was Joe supposed to utter one of the conventional eulogies of the dead that he heard people murmur when they arrived to pay condolences at the deaths of his relatives? He tried to think of one that would be suitable, then he saw to his relief that Sammy did not mean that. It was not of his father when alive that he sought Joe's opinion, but as a corpse. Joe almost said how small he looked, tiny even, and how wonderful it was he had been such a terror, that tiny man, one-time horse trooper, soldier of the Queen, perhaps lusty singer of 'Good-bye Dolly I must leave you though it breaks my heart to go', but instead, muttered hastily that he looked very nice. These few words seemed to satisfy Sammy, indeed to move him deeply. He brushed away some tears with the sleeve of his coat.

Mrs Jackson was seated in the parlour receiving the condolences of callers. What a stranger you are, she said to Joe with that kind of dreamy gentleness which grief and the duties of mourning sometimes confer on widows. She said that she had seen a stranger on the bars of the fire only the day before. Such a big piece of colly on the bars. That must have been you, she told Joe.

Joe wondered at this new aspect of himself as a stranger foretold by burning coals. He tried to think of things to say but all he could think of were the kopees of South Africa and the old horse that had gone for pig meal. He knew by now that the kopees were hills from which the Dutch farmers had sent down a terrible fusillade against regular British soldiers and brought the still burgeoning British Empire to a halt. But none of these things he mentioned, and as soon as he could he took his leave. Forgetting that she had said it already, Mrs Jackson said again that she had seen a dark stranger fluttering black on the grate.

Sammy was cheerful again when they shook hands. The feel of his hands startled Joe. They were so coarse and rough that Joe thought for a moment he was wearing gloves. He thought too for a moment of their sieges and forts on the Boiling Well Meadow, of the Khyber Pass and of the poem 'Hohenlinden'. But when he looked again at Sammy's face he saw that these things were far in the distant past; that of the boy who had once been a proud Zulu warrior, no trace remained.

10

'From each according to his ability; to each according to his need.' Joe once informed the Sunday dinner table that that text from Karl Marx was finer than the Beatitudes of the Sermon on the Mount. No one paid much attention and his mother went on interrogating Mr McCabe on who was at church, who was not, signs of infirmity or recovery, whether Miss So-and-so had that awful hat on in the choir, not a bit *church*, and other church affairs which could only be elicited by shrewd and close questioning. Joe referred to religion as 'the opium of the people' which got a little more attention. Mr McCabe said he wondered about these things sometimes but there was Handel and *The Messiah* ... if it wasn't for the singing ... and Mrs McCabe said scathingly that's right, bring that one up a heathen. But only when he referred to Pope Pius as 'the Arch opium dealer in Rome' did a heated discussion ensue, though more one-sided than he intended. His mother spoke. She would listen to no riff-raff bigotry in *her* house let alone from one of her children ... he would respect Catholics as long as he lived under this roof ... *she* had been brought up to respect Catholics ... as well it wasn't *her* father he said that to. No, no, mother ... didn't mean Protestant bigotry ... churches on side of property ... French Revolution ... Mussolini. *Her* father always said ... *they* have their religion and *we* have ours ... would have taken a stick to a pup like him. Oh be civilised mother! His grandfather would have civilised him all right! With a good slap round the mouth! For God's sake mother ... didn't mean ... usual Orange eff-the-Pope-King-Billy-keep-the-banner-out-of-the-tram-wires-boys.

What! Was his father going to sit there on a Sunday and listen to that foul-mouthed brat of his... mocking decent Orangemen ... *her* father had been an Apprentice Boy and an officer in the Royal Black Institution ... always said *they* have their processions and *we* have ours. No, mother no, mother for God's sake ... completely wrong end! *He* would have wrong-ended you all right! With the handle of a yard brush!

Joe, hurt and outraged at being *misunderstood*, had appealed to the others to help clear his name. But in vain.

Away and start the revolution somewhere else, they said.

Not long after there was a much more momentous occasion on which his mother again referred to Joe as a brat and a pup. It was the 1945 General Election for the Westminster Parliament. Mr McCabe came back after voting and, still marvelling at his own audacity, announced that he had voted Labour! Well! Joe did not play much part in the debates that followed but this did not save him from castigation. When Mr McCabe spoke there seemed to be new notes in the old familiar theme of his discourse: Dead Hand Of Old Fogeyism In Church And State. Need for change. Public ownership. Aneurin Bevan. It's *that pup* his mother said.

The uncle from the Masonic came round. Split the Unionist vote. Different across the water. Vote Labour there and good luck to you. Let the Nationalists in. Would vote Labour himself in England. But the Border. Not sound on the Border. Joe heard his mother tell his aunt that *that brat* had marched that fool of a father of his down to the polling booths! A neighbour woman said she had heard tell of other Protestant men voting Labour, what had got into them, there was one down the street, that wife of his would Labour him if she found out would make up his bed in the parlour, was always doing that to the poor cratur, that or go flying back to the mother, ah God help him you would feel sorry for him a neighbour took him in some stew and he near ate plate and all.

When the election results started coming over the radio Mr McCabe listened in growing excitement as intimations grew of a Labour landslide. Joe would always remember that sunny afternoon and the cool BBC voice reading out the state of the parties. Bristol: Labour. Islington: Labour. The BBC man became almost monotonous in his litany of Labour victories. Labour. Labour. Labour. Mr McCabe kept coming in from the garden where he was dibbling leeks until Mrs McCabe threatened to lock him out. Either dig your garden or cheer on the election, look what you're bringing in on your feet. But he was too excited to do either calmly and he was heard in the garden shouting the latest count to somebody over the hedge. But will they have an overall majority? Ramsay MacDonald. Sad business. But the BBC man in his Oxford accent left no doubt. Labour was sweeping the country. The dead hand of old fogeyism in church and state was being dealt a mortal blow. His mother and the neighbour women said poor Winston Churchill. Won the war for us and now look at the thanks he gets!

Joe wandered the streets excited and sensed excitement everywhere. It was a strange kind of excitement, subdued, not alluded to – there weren't many like his father – but detectable as an undercurrent in the casual remarks and matter-of-fact voices, an awareness that something big was happening and a wonder as to what it would mean. He would never forget that bright day: his father brandishing the leek dibbler at the radio; the BBC man saying Mr Clement Attlee; the consternation of true-blue diehards; men in a shop speaking of Keir Hardie and the first working men in Parliament; an old man at the hedge with his father recalling the time of the first old age pension under Asquith and Lloyd George; his own feeling that, even if the Northern Ireland Labour men had not done so well nevertheless the great tide of change in England would wash over them and somehow or other melt away all that rubbish of *them* with their religion and *us* with ours; *their* days; *our* days; Kevin Barry; Derry's Walls; the Easter Rising; No Pope Here. The old ones might be a lost cause but how could the young think that bog-peasant parish pump brawling important after years of *big* stuff. Dunkirk. Stalingrad. Roosevelt. We will fight on the beaches. The Gas Chambers. The Atom Bomb on Hiroshima. That song seemed to sum it up.

'How ya gonna keep 'em down on the farm after they've seen Paree?' Mr McCabe might have expressed it rather differently with different words. Mr McCabe loved words. His religious stance of near-unbelief tempered by love of church music was not quite true. He also loved the words. The great words of the King James Version of the Protestant Bible. Sometimes instead of being heard softly singing bits of psalms or *The Messiah* to himself he would be heard softly speaking the words in a reflective sort of way as if listening to them and musing upon them. *Every valley shall be exalted, and every mountain and hill shall be made low.* It was not clear when Mr McCabe murmured those words to himself at that time around the house or in the garden if he did so merely from long habit or if he consciously saw in the words of Isaiah a more sonorous phrasing of the jubilation of the British Labour Party: *We* are the masters now.

But. Time passed. Life went on. The 1945 Election itself became absorbed into the past. As to great tides, well, Joe wandered once or twice through the huge American army camp now derelict and tried to read the names cut in the inside of a sentry box. Those odd American names, odd American places. Delphis, Mo. They liked you to have a sister if you turned up at their Christmas parties, but they let you in anyway. Row upon row of empty Nissen huts some with doors missing. The War had been the great tide and it had receded. Life resumed its old daily round.

In the market square General Nicholson still stood upon his plinth, the great soldier-Christian hero of Lucknow and Cawnpore, upraised sabre still in one hand, pistol in the other, beckoning all to follow him *onward* and *upward*. Men as of yore went in and out of the public houses and the bookies, others accompanied the wife round the shops to see where the money went, young matrons blocked the thoroughfares with prams like galleons just to put the baby on show, and Sticky Sloan, the doorman of the Picture House still, as in time immemorial, marshalled the waiting queues to stop them leaning against the window of Fusco's fish and chip saloon with appropriate gestures of his white gloved hand. And, as Mrs McCabe and the neighbour women could have predicted, only the men never listened to them, *they* still had *their* days and *we* had *ours*. Kevin Barry and Derry's Walls and the Easter Rising and No Pope Here.

11

As he stepped out of his front door Mr McCabe gave his bowler hat a last brush with his cuff before settling it on his head. The funeral of his cousin James Tiley, otherwise known as Dancer, was from the house at half-past two. Mr McCabe was a seasoned mourner with many funerals behind him of every description: wet and dry; big turnouts and small; slow black horse and coach affairs; fast motor ones; funerals that marked the end of epochs and funerals of not the slightest significance; summer funerals when the black suit was sticking to you and winter ones when the wind went through you like a knife and blew away the words intoned by the minister at the graveside that anyway they all knew by heart: 'Man that is born of a woman hath but a short time to live, and is full of misery...'

Mr McCabe's rosy cheeks were smoothly shaved and his bearing manly. His grave though cheerful demeanour showed nothing of the effort and vexation which it had cost his wife and daughter to get him ready, each with their parts to play – some demanding great acumen and tact – in handing him articles of clothing or adornment at the right moment to stop him ransacking and plundering looking for them, or seeing that all his buttons were properly done up before he presented himself to the public gaze. Although the first-born of a large family, Mr McCabe had been on his mother's and his sisters' hands till he was nearly forty and consequently accepted being waited on hand and foot by a household of women as part of the natural scheme of things. Nothing of these preparations or of the household disorder resulting from them was visible as he saluted neighbour women with a smiling courtesy in which there was an awareness of himself – unconscious perhaps – as a fine figure of a man despite his years. He walked in a purposeful arm-swinging military fashion that was not especially suitable for busy streets when accompanied. Joe, as well as having trouble keeping up with his father, had often to stand aside to let people pass and even to dodge about from one side of him to the other in order for both of them to get through the crowded thoroughfares without collision.

James Tiley had been the champion boxer of the British Army in the lightweight class. He had later turned professional though only for a brief brilliant career which, wisely, ended on a note of glory when he went twelve rounds with Spider Nelson, British Empire champion. Even though defeated he was carried home in triumph through the streets because of the honour he had done the city. It was said that the bookmakers had made a fortune from so much local money being put on him purely from sentiment and people often spoke of the terrible beating he had taken not to let the city down.

Though the fame of this faded with the years it was kept alive among the children of his locality when they saw Spider Nelson on the cigarette cards they collected in the 'Famous Boxers' series and then they would mention his name, greatly to the satisfaction of children like Joe who were related to him. He was nicknamed 'Dancer' from having tiny feet slightly turned in which gave him a distinctive walk, at once both lumbering and delicate. He seemed to move to some secret music with a kind of clumsy grace.

He was a rigger, though the children preferred the title of steeplejack as connoting something more daring and romantic. His work took him up great heights, to the tops of buildings, masts, church spires, mill chimneys. There was a mill chimney seen from the classrooms of his old school, The Free, which the children for a time firmly believed was climbed by Dancer every night to light a lamp at the top for warning aeroplanes. From certain of the desks the chimney appeared in a window framing a scene which might have been a picture entitled 'The Mill' and this, like Spider Nelson on the cigarette cards, tended by association to allow his legend faintly to survive into another generation.

As Joe and his father made their way to Dancer's house a gypsy-looking woman with coils of greying hair greeted Mr McCabe by his first name.

'Good day Mrs Coulter,' Mr McCabe saluted her with cheerful gravity.

She began telling them without preamble or reserve where she was going and why. It was to get a picture mended that her old dog had knocked over and broken the glass. She rummaged in her bag and produced a framed photo of a soldier, though his cap and tunic showed that he belonged to a bygone age. She was about to tell them all about it when she suddenly noticed Mr McCabe's bowler hat and asked him who was dead.

'Ah Christ poor Dancer,' she said when he told her, and then she wondered angrily why nobody could have let her know. She said she could have sworn she had seen Dancer in the distance only the week before when she was coming out of the bookies to put half-a-crown on Dawn Chorus and she had thought he was better. She did a little imitation of the lightly springing walk of the figure she had taken for Dancer and then looked at Mr McCabe in awe.

'Was that a sign?' she asked sharply and Mr McCabe said he wouldn't know about such things but said it with a sigh to show that he kept an open mind. Did he know what *she* thought had killed Dancer? Joe thought she was going to say cancer but she said *marriage*, referring to the fact that Dancer had married a widow very late in life – though very enthusiastically, scandalously so, some thought for a man of his age.

'A man like Dancer,' she said indignantly, 'living on his own all those years, how could it not affect the constitution.'

Joe remembered Dancer bringing him to his house almost by force to see how well he was taking to the married state. He had watched Joe eat his wife's cakes with open eagerness for him to say how good they were. He sat watching Joe eat with shining eyes, his hands on his knees and his small dainty feet tucked under the chair, nodding at him interrogatively with beaming smiles, inviting him to share in the wonder of *him*, even him, Dancer Tiley, being a married man, able to stage such a scene of blissful domesticity.

But Mrs Coulter's tone when she blamed Dancer's death on marriage had something in it which hinted at quite other things than cakes and cookery. Mr McCabe doubted this as gently as he could without offending her, but Mrs Coulter went on to criticise Dancer's late marriage more openly. What about all his boxing stuff, she demanded. What about the framed boxing pictures that her man had been in along with Dancer? She made a bonfire of all that boxing stuff, Mrs Coulter accused, pictures and all. There were children, said Mrs Coulter, pointing with an upraised arm in the direction they were heading, there were children nearly had their eyes put out from poking that bonfire that she put the boxing pictures on with the glass still in them. She wouldn't let any of his old boxing crowd near him when he took ill, Mrs Coulter claimed angrily, she put them out if they called.

Mr McCabe explained to her that it wasn't only the

boxing crowd that had been kept away but the Gospel Hall people as well that he had been very thick with for a time. The Gospel Hall people had wanted, said Mr McCabe, to hold a prayer meeting round his bed and she had put them out. The even-handedness of this seemed to mollify Mrs Coulter, indeed to give her a certain satisfaction and she returned to the earlier grievance of why nobody had bothered to let her know that Dancer was dead. Did Mr McCabe know why that was? She asked the question in a rhetorical tone. She would tell him for why. It was because, she told him with an air of bitter shrewdness, that she didn't tell the people her business. It was telling the people her business that had been her ruin and she had learnt her lesson. Dancer, God help him, had always been on at her to stop telling the people her business. That time when they took the widow's pension off her and Dancer had filled in the papers for the appeal he had said, Mamie, he said, you'll have to stop telling the people your business. God help poor Dancer that should never have married. Sure it was well known that boxers daren't go near women!

'Mrs Coulter,' said Mr McCabe with a smile, 'there are only two classes of people you tell your business to: the people that ask you' (here he paused slightly to give effect to the rest), 'and the people that don't!'

For a moment Joe thought with alarm that his father was being too free. Mrs Coulter had a reputation for letting fly abusive language at people who offended her. He carried a memory from childhood of an elderly well-dressed man being turned upon by Mrs Coulter when he went to remonstrate with the man who was beating her outside a public house. He could still remember the dismay upon the man's pale face as he hurried away pursued by Mrs Coulter's jeers in which there was the same note of something indecent as when she denounced Dancer's wife for marrying him. Did his father want them humiliated in the street? But Mr McCabe knew her better than his son thought, for after a moment when she seemed startled by what he said, she threw her head back and gave a great cackle of laughter in which for a moment or two he joined, clearly pleased with what he had said, till he remembered his dark suit and bowler hat and said that they would have to be on their way. People who paused to look at Mrs Coulter in her merriment at Mr McCabe's witty quip hurried on when, even as she was laughing, she met their looks with a bold glare. She reached for her purse and asked Mr McCabe if the lad there, meaning Joe, could get a bunch of flowers for her to take to Dancer's funeral. Mr McCabe said with a sigh that it would not be proper, which she conceded. As they moved away she called out defiantly that she'd get a flower to put on Dancer's grave when all *their* wreaths were withered.

The people that ask you and the people that don't, Mr McCabe repeated to himself as they walked on through the busy shoppers, savouring again his wit with satisfaction. Joe asked his father about Mrs Coulter's connection with Dancer. Was her man a boxer? Mr McCabe said that the man she had at that time was one of the boxing crowd that went with him every place he fought. You would hardly know what they were all for, he told his son musingly. There was one to slip in the gumshield. There was one to give him sips to drink. One to sponge him down. Mr McCabe said that when he had been out training on the roads they were round him like flies on bicycles. Mr McCabe concluded sadly that it was most probably the drink they were after.

Several of Mr McCabe's sisters were at Dancer's house to help, for there were few women in the Tiley connection. Some powerful strain of maleness asserted itself no matter whom they married and they produced only sons. Hence, when there were funerals, people had to show them what to do regarding the proprieties and customs for it is, after all, only women who are good with death. Dancer's wife was too grief-stricken to do more than greet the mourners tearfully and it was one of the other women who whispered at the men sitting in the parlour with bowler hats on their knees if they would take a glass of brandy. One of the men, another cousin of Mr McCabe, who had been in the Irish Guards, the Black and Tans, and the Royal Ulster Constabulary and was still called Sergeant Tiley, asked with a laugh had she not a glass for Joe too but his father said he'd be time enough in a year or two.

Sergeant Tiley had carried over into civilian life a faculty to assume command. He held a discreet discussion with the undertaker on the route to be taken. The men nursing their bowler hats and their warmers of brandy heard words fall, soft but decisive, as they reached agreement. Nothing like the old style funerals. But the traffic nowadays. Very sad. People still set their hearts on being walked through the streets at the finish but the police didn't like it. Drive him part of the way. The Rialto picture house. Would walk him from the Rialto.

Soon the word spread to the men waiting outside that they were going to walk Dancer from the Rialto.

Sergeant Tiley cast an appraising eye at the turnout of mourners as they left the house, and again when the motors stopped after the first stage which aroused indignation in some because of its unseemly haste but was accepted sadly as a sign of the times by most. Sergeant Tiley began recruiting the pall-bearers.

Joe knew from the way that they had joked about giving him a glass of brandy that Sergeant Tiley would pick him for a turn and as they walked slowly in the huge cortege that contained many men he was more used to seeing outside public houses and bookies, some of the men with

117

battered faces, he waited for it to come. Sergeant Tiley strolled back along the column, falling quietly into step to have a word in a man's ear and the man would make his way to the front to be ready for the next change of pall-bearers. He stopped at where Mr McCabe was and said, not to Joe but to his father, 'would the lad there give Dancer a lift'.

Sergeant Tiley and the undertaker's man held the coffin while each pair of men changed. Joe felt the edge settle down hard on his shoulder and he did what he was told, to put his arm round the shoulder of the man beside him and to take his step from him. Sergeant Tiley's hand was still under the coffin as, apprehensively, he took the first step praying that nothing awful would happen. Nothing did. There seemed to be transmitted through the coffin the rhythm of the step of the other experienced men. Sergeant Tiley's hand withdrew. Away you go, he said approvingly. Joe felt a surge of pride at doing something only men do. He was a boy no longer. He returned to his father in a glow of self-satisfaction and he listened to the men around them talk of other funerals and of how far they had had to carry the dead, with the complacent understanding of experience.

After the funeral when they sat again in the parlour, now less solemn, with the blinds raised and a return to everyday voices and casual manners, surprise was again expressed when Sergeant Tiley again refused a drink as he had before the funeral. He hadn't touched it for a year he said and Mr McCabe said he was amazed to hear it. Sergeant Tiley said that he had stopped smoking too for a while, otherwise the doctors would have given him up. I see that you are back on the cigarettes though, said Mr McCabe enquiringly, prompting him to tell them why. The doctor made me, said Sergeant Tiley, when I went back to him in a terrible state after four months without a drink or a smoke. You gave up too much, the doctor said, the constitution won't stand it. So he went back on the cigarettes. But not the drink, said Mr McCabe admiringly, and seemingly for answer Sergeant Tiley held before them an outstretched hand that was now as steady as a rock.

The men spoke in awe of the mysteries of the human constitution and what could upset it, and Mr McCabe mentioned his encounter with Mrs Coulter and her theory that marriage could damage the constitution of men not used to it at which there was a shout of laughter all round.

'Mrs Coulter,' said Mr McCabe, 'is a woman that didn't go in much for marriage herself.'

'She promoted me,' said Sergeant Tiley. He waggled his bulk from the hips and mimicked a woman's voice saying with outrageous brazen flattery, ' "a woman asked me only the other day if that man Tiley hadn't been an *officer* in the army he walks that straight and upright." '

As he was telling this he got out his cigarettes and was handing them round just as Mrs McCabe appeared. When he came to Joe he hesitated, then with a half-contemptuous half-affectionate gesture he flung a cigarette to the floor for him to pick up and light right in front of his father and mother for the first time. Like being picked as a pall-bearer, it was a further token that he was being received into the company of men. He listened critically and impatiently as his father related his little triumph of wit about Mrs Coulter keeping her business to herself. *People that ask you ... and people that don't.* He was embellishing it as he told it. The pause had got longer and more effective. It might have been an anecdote from the sayings of a famous man and Mr McCabe spoke the telling phrases as if they too were famous. He doubled up with laughter and slapped his thigh.

His son Joe smoked his first public cigarette and reflected

with satisfaction that, like shouldering Dancer's coffin, it was a signal of his impending manhood. Emboldened by the thought of that, he dared to claim a share in the man's talk about Mrs Coulter.

'The merry widow,' he said with a laugh, which, when it came out, sounded more knowing than he intended and made him want to take it back in case it earned a rebuke and spoilt the good feeling of the cigarette, of being a boy no longer, of having borne the dead upon his shoulder, of having carried a warrior honoured of his tribe to his last resting place. But to his relief they let it pass.

'She was a fine looking woman in her day,' said Mr McCabe gravely with a sigh.

'Oh a right armful,' said Sergeant Tiley with shrewd appreciativeness though looking first with exaggerated care to see that none of the women would overhear him, at which they all laughed.

'Such a squad of children,' said Mr McCabe, 'I never knew whose they all were. God help us all, she would hardly know herself.'

'Oh I think she would,' said Sergeant Tiley judiciously. 'Women always know.'

'Young Cissie Coulter,' said Joe suddenly, recovering his boldness, 'who was *her* father?' He thought of the little girl he had gone to school with and of all the years of childhood when he had been unaware of what had gone before and utterly incurious. Even now it was more the fact of being included in such a conversation that interested him rather than the things they spoke of.

'Not guilty sir,' cried Sergeant Tiley with mock outrage and then in an amused tone added, 'You'll have to be careful where you ask that question.'

'She was very thick with Dancer at one time,' said one of the other men, not looking at Sergeant Tiley but clearly hoping to prompt some significant comment, but Sergeant Tiley remained silent and his expression was inscrutable.

'The time of the big fight,' said Mr McCabe, 'she went to London along with the rest. Such a boatload of hangers-on.'

'She seemed to have collected one or two more when they got back,' said Sergeant Tiley, who had been at the docks when the Liverpool boat arrived. He mentioned briefly what was well known to them all: the crowds to carry Dancer shoulder high and the brass band to accompany the triumphal procession. Then in more lively tones he described Mrs Coulter coming down the gangplank.

'Like a Queen,' said Sergeant Tiley, 'men all round her. Men carrying things for her. There was these two gentlemen from the first class carrying stuff for her along with the rest of them.' Sergeant Tiley changed his voice and his accent to indicate how well-spoken the two gentlemen were and he made a little fastidious tugging movement at the lapels of his coat to imply the gentlemanly quality of their clothes though he could not refrain from breaking into a laugh as he told what they were carrying.

'One of them,' he said, 'had a gramophone that was bought for her in London, and the other gentleman had a parcel of pigs' feet that she had got hold of in Liverpool.'

'She loved pigs' feet,' said the man who had tried in vain to elicit an authoritative version of her relations with Dancer. 'There was nothing she loved better than a feed of pigs' feet – so hard to get nowadays the shops don't sell them.'

'Oh not just nowadays,' said Sergeant Tiley, 'pigs' feet shopkeepers were a dying race twenty years ago. I mind one night we were on patrol up round the Falls Road at the time of the riots when the IRA shot Chief Constable Blake coming out of church, just after the curfew was lifted. Our Crossley armoured car turned a corner near

Sandy Row and there was this woman hurrying along with a parcel. Says I to her from the back of the Crossley is that you Mamie Coulter just as well I knew you from behind you might have got yourself shot what's that you're carrying? Pigs' feet, she says, Sandy Row is the only place left in Belfast on a Saturday night that has them. The craving come over me, she says, I love to suck on the bones.'

Joe puffed ostentatiously at his cigarette as the glasses of all the men except Sergeant Tiley were discreetly replenished. There was something in the way the others sippcd their drinks that was a faint gesture of admiration for his strong-willed abstinence.

Joe wanted to participate again in their talk, yet the subject matter made him uneasy. Though he was at that age when thoughts about women were often in his mind, he felt uncomfortable with the idea that such things had ever touched the lives of his parents' generation who to him had always been old and he did not want to try to imagine them otherwise. He glanced covertly at the ageing men around him and at the women who put their heads round the door, at their sagging bodies and ruined looks, while his mind not only resisted the idea that they could ever have been visited by lust and passion but rejected it with distaste, indeed incredulity. He suddenly thought of the face he had caught a glimpse of on the photograph that Mrs Coulter had pulled out of her bag to show them before she saw his father's bowler hat and suit of mourning clothes. He remembered seeing the face of someone young and handsome. A young good-looking soldier in an old-fashioned peaked cap. He was about to ask them who it was when his aunt came to summon them to their tea and he was willing to let it slip from his mind. In any case he did not want to make the effort of trying to connect a strikingly handsome young man with a stout quarrelsome woman who had a flutter on the horses and took a glass of something to lift her mind. To him youth could belong only to youth. The forms and identities of the older people around him he could not think of as other than coming into existence ready-made when he was born. He did not want to think of what had gone before as anything more than a misty void from which tales came. The idea that he might ever become as they were, preoccupied with their bodies' ailments, with food, money, drink, cures, was unthinkable, it simply could not enter his head.

Then he heard his father mention the photograph and he listened to them talk about it. Died in the First World War. Mrs Coulter's man. Which one? Might have been the best one God help him. Would have told you all about the photo when you met her on the street if you had had the time. At the top of her voice! A very superstitious woman. Would hear the name of a horse in something you might say to her and take that as a Sign to back it. That soldier on the photo would be the father of the oldest one. Told me once *I* gave her the Derby winner only she didn't heed the Sign! Would that be his son, the singer one, would hear him in the Horse Shoe Bar on a Saturday night. Lily of Laguna.

As he half-listened some lines of verse came into Joe's head, some that he deliberately and rather solemnly thought about, others unbidden. The first kind was from the poem recited on Remembrance Day about them not growing old: *Age shall not weary them, nor the years condemn.* But the other lines he could not place where he had learnt them. *Who passes by this road so late, always gay.* Something to do with knights. Was it from the King Arthur legends? *Of all the Queen's Knights he was the flower, always gay.* The Knights of the Round Table? Queen Guinevere? Sir Gawain. Sir Lancelot. Sergeant Tiley. Dancer. The young soldier. What an idea!

Fat Mrs Coulter as Guinevere! And who was the one that went off in search of the Holy Grail to prove his love? Sir Galahad? He would have to look it tip. Next time he was in Smithfield he would look for something on the Knights of the Round Table in the second-hand bookshops. *Of all the Queen's Knights he was the flower.* The line was all mixed up in his head with thoughts about being a boy no longer, about all his life being in front of him, of life opening all its doors to him, full of infinite possibilities, and he went at the ham tea with gusto, almost oblivious of how much he was enjoying it.

The old framed photograph, sepia coloured and faded, was of a young soldier long dead. He had died in the First World War. His thin delicate face was quite beautiful. People felt no embarrassment at saying how beautiful he looked. But they said it not so much admiringly as pityingly. Some said it in that way even before they learnt he had died young, so much did it seem the face of one too fine and delicate to last.

Had he been killed in action? No. He never reached the front line. He fell ill on the troop train taking him there and died in hospital. His body was sent back to Belfast for burial.

He had a full military funeral in Belfast, though it was explained to his young widow Mrs Coulter that she could have had a lump sum of ten pounds had she chosen not to have what she afterwards referred to as 'the cart', meaning the gun carriage with full escort. But she had resisted the pressures on her to do that and had never regretted it. The streets were all out to watch his funeral pass by.

She had been helped with all the formalities by Dr Harrison, then an army surgeon who happened to be on leave at the time. Captain Harrison, as he then was, had been shocked and angry that the soldier had been allowed to set off in such a sick condition. He would never have allowed it if he had known. When Mrs Coulter recounted the things that Dr Harrison said at that time she gave the impression of a man much milder of speech than he became in later life when it would not have been possible to report him truthfully without at least indicating some of the cursing for which he became notorious. Dr Harrison stumped the wards of the infirmary as if it were a casualty station on the Western Front; even in his surgery he gave offence to women patients who often signed on with other doctors, leaving him husbands and sons better fitted to put up with his damning and helling, his bloody this and his bloody that. But then Dr Harrison had been a young man himself, and probably not in the least like the burly red-faced man who marched with the ex-servicemen on Remembrance Day, swinging his arms very high.

Why had she not got the doctor to him when he took ill on his last leave from the training camp? Mrs Coulter said he wouldn't let her. Oh he wouldn't hear of it! Captain Harrison had wanted to kick up a fuss with the Army authorities as to how a man with bad lungs could ever have been passed by the doctors at the recruiting station. He should never have been in the Army at all. Why hadn't she done something about it? What possessed him to enlist in the first place?

He enlisted so that he could marry her, Mrs Coulter explained. It was because of her father, she said. Her father was dead set against him because of his bad chest. Her father put him out of the house when he came round courting her. Insulted them if he met them together on the streets. On one occasion he had to kneel down in the middle of a crowd of mill girls as her father turned the corner and passed them unsuspecting – skirts were long in those days and he was a lightly built lad. But her father kept catching them together and when he did he insulted him.

Away and take your TB somewhere else, her father told him! Imagine saying the like of that to him. It preyed on his mind. He once threw himself into the mill-race in despair and they brought him to her half-dead on a hand-cart. Mrs Coulter would relate this episode with great feeling, looking sternly at each of her listeners in turn to make sure that they were fully aware of its drama and were properly affected. *Away and take your TB somewhere else.*

Not but what, she would then add in a very different tone, casual, reasonable, anxious to be fair to the memory of her father, not but what all that family was in fact rotten with consumption.

That was why he enlisted. Why? Oh well because her father couldn't insult him then. Oh her father daren't insult the uniform! There was nothing her father could do after that to stop them getting married. Her father daren't insult the uniform!

It was Captain Harrison who had advised Mrs Coulter about the lump sum option in lieu of the full military funeral. But she had been adamant. All the streets were out and the people were at all the windows. She was equally adamant that there was nothing she could have done to stop him going back from leave with a fever on him.

He wouldn't, she said proudly, give my father the satisfaction.

Oh no, she would repeat solemnly, again looking her listeners sternly in the eye to see that the inevitability of it was impressed upon them. He wouldn't give her father the satisfaction.

But if she never regretted not taking Dr Harrison's

advice about the money option instead of what she called the 'cart', she did regret – sometimes – not taking it about other matters. Dr Harrison, she conceded with a sigh, had given her good advice, but she had been young and foolish. When he had got all the formalities settled for her war widow's pension he told her to take care.

'Now look here Mamie,' he said, '*you behave yourself* or they'll take it off you.'

So the time came when they did indeed take away her war widow's pension. Perhaps she had it longer than Dr Harrison would have thought, if indeed he thought about it at all when he became the stout rough-spoken doctor they all knew so well who was mocked by the little boys for the way he marched with the ex-servicemen. The little boys would march leaning back so far they nearly fell over and swinging their arms ridiculously high in imitation of him.

But though she had had her fling since then, and, in between the hard times, been on many a binge, many a right royal spree, none of her men ever quite took the place of the beautiful young soldier who had been her only proper husband and for so short a time. When his picture got knocked down and damaged at a party for American soldiers in the Second World War she had it expensively restored and it was thenceforth put safely out of harm's way at all her soirées.

When people looked at the picture and said how beautiful he was she would sigh and perhaps even shed a tear. For there was a time, oh there was a time, when she had been as lovely as a flower, and a beautiful young lover with the face of a poet had died for love of her and been borne to his grave with pomp and ceremony on a gun carriage draped with the flag through the streets of his native city, lined with silent people filled with pity and with awe.

12

There came upon him this longing to walk to the sea, to walk through the city till he came to a road that would take him to the sea. And then? He was not sure. Perhaps simply walk on and let the sea close over him. The impulse had come to him in the night and had filled him with strange feelings in which there was both sadness and excitement. The thought that at last he was doing something decisive gladdened him because whatever happened at the sea everything afterwards would be changed. His spirits rose as he lay thinking where would be the best for his purpose. He wanted no muddy creeks, no promenades, no ice-cream parlours, no tin-roofed bungalows, but just the sea and the wide sky and a gentle sloping shore. So he would not go out along the busy Belfast Lough on either shore but would head south. He liked the idea of *south*. It held a promise of warmth and escape. The idea of *south* was still in his mind the next morning so that he asked his mother to put an orange in his lunch.

As he walked through the city streets towards a southern road the thought of eating his orange by a quiet place on the way to the sea brightened the dark shadow cast by the thought that he might never return.

Yet his state of mind did not in the least prevent him from taking a lively interest in the passing scene of busy city life as he made his way to the Saintfield Road towards Carryduff, Ballynahinch, Dundrum, Newcastle and the sea. He looked with wistful pleasure at all the fleeting images of morning bustle that came constantly before his eyes as he walked.

He cut through the back streets around Taylor's Mill. The streets all had names commemorating our great Imperial past. Blenheim Street. Bengal Street. Trafalgar Street. Quebec Street. He paused to watch the sweating packers trundle onto the loading bay of the mill bales and crates on which were painted boldly the names of the great cities and sea-ports of the world.

Yokahama! Use No Hooks! Valparaiso via Panama! The impatient packers called out the names of distant cities in tones of urgency, often with anger, sometimes with curses. Bombay! Copenhagen! Vera Cruz! The foreman packer stood imperturbable in his flat cap and muffler like some latter day Apollo and calmly assigned the bales and crates each to its appointed place in order to be despatched swiftly to the ends of the earth.

The feeling of disesteem for himself was renewed. He had been nowhere. He had done nothing. How could women ever love one so insubstantial, so shadowy.

Vera Cruz. Villa Rica de la Vera Cruz. He knew that to be its full name. Rich town of the true cross. Where the Conquistadors had first caught sight of Aztec gold.

He wished he was someone who had returned from somewhere with a celebrated name. Not every foreign place would do. He saw on the crates and bales of the loading bay the names of places like Winnipeg, Auckland, Melbourne. He tried the sound of them in his mind for the merit of having been to them. No ring to them. None whatsoever. Not like Samarkand. Sarajevo. Ur of the Chaldees.

He thought how wonderful life was if only it could be reached. It was not life he was turning away from, far from it, but rather from his inability to pierce its armour, his total failure to be part of it, his tormenting exclusion from it. If he kept walking until he came to the sea and then perhaps on and on, he might one way or another break out of his glass prison.

Just before he moved on from the mill a lift came clanking down near the loading bay. A notice threatened dire consequences against unauthorised persons riding in it. *For Goods Only. Will Be Instantly Dismissed.* The notice belonged to a harsher age but a more confident one for it was cast in iron. *To The Stairs* said the iron words, pointing sternly with an iron hand, confident that the rule of iron would endure for ever. Yet a bevy of laughing girls rushed into the lift blithely disregarding not only the words of iron but the feeble protests of the old liftman who said that they would get him into trouble so many of them. We wouldn't get you into trouble, they assured him, same as you wouldn't like to get us into trouble, they chorused at him sweetly with such innuendo that there was an outbreak of sniggering.

Joe watched the vivacious girls being cut off from him by the clashing steel gates and borne swiftly away in their steel cage. Yet it seemed to him as if he were in the cage, not they, and that the bars were of his own timidity. He seemed held fast in a cage of impregnable timidity round which life moved, tantalisingly, alluringly, and he thought that he could bear it no longer.

When he got back late that night they wanted to know where he had been.

Nowhere, he said.

His mother said not to tell lies. Such a habit he had got into, she claimed, telling lies. Nowhere! Nobody! Nothing! was all people could get out of him. Not as if, she said angrily, he had parents like *some*. Had to know everything about sons his age, let alone daughters. Had to know who? where? when? And you would have to be in by a set time every night, all your letters opened, not so much as a Christmas card that wouldn't be opened, how would he like that? But they, she said, speaking also for his father, they believed in trust, though not if it was abused, like that letter that had come for him from that Steamship Company in London and not one word could they get out of him what he was doing enquiring the price of tickets to South America! Did he not know that his chums had called wanting to know where he was? Mr Laffin had called that he was supposed to do the books for to pay the men. What was all this disappearing about? All this moping and sulking? And books! books! books! He wouldn't have an eye left in his head from reading. What did he want to do, what did he want to be, they asked him resentfully. Why could he not be a credit to his parents like the others?

He did not know. He listened without rancour or scorn or even disapproval to the others' eager talk of examinations, credits, distinctions, bursaries, scholarships, honours degrees, masters' degrees, Arts and Sciences, Electrical, Mechanical, Civil, of people who were at Queen's, of daughters at Stranmillis, of others waiting in trepidation to be called before boards, panels, selection committees, applications in triplicate, canvassing would disqualify.

His uncle said whatever he did be sure to get the qualifications first. Oh get your Certificates first. His uncle pronounced certificates with the emphasis on the first syllable. He personally, his uncle said tolerantly, would not think less of a lad that wanted to knock about a bit, rough it for a while – ay and maybe get his hands dirty – before he settled down. As long as he had the CERTificates to fall back on – he could dig ditches if he liked. He was never done telling them down at the Masonic that it was lads with a bit of spirit and adventure in them that had made this Great Empire of ours in the first place. His uncle always smacked his fist down on his palm when he spoke of what he told the Masonic was the secret of the Empire.

But Joe said nothing. He had failed. He did not like to think of how he had become tired of walking, of finding nowhere to rest and eat his lunch that contained an orange because of hedges, houses, barred gates, figures turning to look; of cheating by climbing on a bus, of sitting in a fish and chip shop with his orange still in his pocket.

How different the countryside was to what it seemed in his memory of that wonderful summer Sunday when they had had such fun with those lovely silly girls on the beach, and in the sea, and on the train coming home. Then the country lay all golden in the setting sun with the mountains all around and the little train wound its way back to Belfast through little whitewashed halts without a platform where the guard let the people on and off with steps, and they all leaned out of the windows to see the business with the steps and call out things at the girls who leaned out of the window of the next compartment. The cool lordly mountains, the motion of the little train in the cool of the evening, the fellows singing songs in close harmony, the girls calling back saucy remarks, the fields glowing in the sunset, all inspired in him a happiness that was astonishing from it being made up of such simple ingredients that it seemed sure to happen any time they liked. They sang songs. The old songs, the latest hits. 'Nellie Dean'. 'A long long trail awinding into the land of my dreams'. Their singing seemed poignant yet filled him with joy. Never had he so envied singers their power to move our hearts. How rich life suddenly seemed; life's riches seemed suddenly there for the taking, you had only to stretch out your hand. Yes, he thought, we will do this more often. So this is Youth, he had exulted. At last he was come into his inheritance, at last he was in the promised land.

> Give me land, lots of land
> Under starry skies above.
> Don't fence me in...
> Let me wander over yonder
> Till I see the mountains rise

And they would be young for years and years! And it would be all like this!

So it had seemed. So much so that it had been with only the lightest of pangs of regret that he had watched the little band of girls troop out of the train at Lurgan, playfully calling out each other's names and addresses, and the fellows doing nothing about it, telling each other scornfully that they weren't going to bloody Lurgan for bloody women! If perhaps it had occurred to him that *he* would, and further than Lurgan maybe, such lovely silly girls they were, he had dismissed the thought lightly. There would be other golden days like that, now he was in the golden time of youth.

But it was not so. There were, it is true, other Sundays that summer when it seemed as if it might happen, when the fellows sauntered idly or loitered bored at a corner, when, for a moment, it seemed as if it might need just a casually uttered suggestion to spark off the same spontaneous urge, joyful and reckless, that would lead again to splashing in the sea with shrieking girls; towering blue mountains; songs old and new sung sweetly at evening time; a quaint swaying train; the faces of laughing girls shining in the setting sun.

It never happened again.

After he tried to walk to the sea he tried to write a poem about that Sunday. But the poem would not come right till he made the standpoint that of age and experience. It was necessary for the seaside branch line to have long closed. The poem began to come right, when, in his mind,

133

he saw only fading marks on the grass where the rails had been. He liked the symbolism of grass growing where once life had been vigorous and gay: urban life, full of bustle, machinery and women. *Weed-grown the little railway line,* he wrote with satisfaction at the idea it was bound to convey of decay and human brevity. *Soon faded the friendships/ Soon chilled was youth's glow* was another bit which seemed fully to justify the hours spent on it. But the words he was most proud of in his rather long poem were to do with the sun. *How soon we crossed that golden plain/ That lay in the sunlight long ago.*

He carried the poem about with him for months, hoping vaguely for an opportunity to arise that would allow him to produce it in company in the most perfectly natural way, for people to read and admire. But then he grew irritated at the way it bulged out his wallet. It began to fray at the folds. Just before he threw away the grubby disintegrating sheets of paper he read it for the last time, no longer admiringly, but impatiently, critically, coldly. He noticed suddenly that he had left out the girls! Those stupid prick-teasing bitches from bloody Lurgan. Yet for a moment before he threw away the silly poem he saw something again in his memory that made his heart yearn: a picture of girls' faces leaning from the window of a swaying train, framed by the mountains and the sky, shining in the golden rays of the evening sun.

13

He carried a snapshot of her in his wallet for a long time. Sometimes he would show it to fellows but only in circumstances when he could do so in a casual off-hand way such as when fellows were showing each other photos of the girls they were going out with and he could copy their manner of faintly amused resentment at being lured by a bit of skirt away from more serious interests and pursuits. Yet the truth was that he loved her so passionately that his heart leapt when he heard people speak her name.

When she had given him a little snapshot of herself he had been too overjoyed to read at once the inscription she had written on the back and anyway her mother had been looking on. Her mother had said with a laugh 'That's Daddy's girl', meaning the way her father showed off what a lovely daughter he had. What she had written on the back was *with best wishes from your friend*. Every time he read it he felt afresh his bitter disappointment on first seeing those words, so cool, so unromantic, acknowledging only friendship, omitting even his name or hers.

He was invited to her seventeenth birthday party and at first his spirits rose when her mother greeted him with a warm hug and said: *this is the one I like*, but then he saw that it also meant how many admirers she had. One of the other fellows chaffed her mother boldly when she teased him about starting work in the manager's office of a mill.

That's no way to speak to a thousand-a-year man, he said with mock severity, and they all laughed heartily except Joe. It filled him with dismay.

After the birthday party he daydreamed about impressing her. He felt that his only hope lay in impressing her, though his daydreams were very vague about what he could do. In his daydreams he was never alone with her. The birthday party crowd was there as well, so were her father and mother, and of course the thousand-a-year man, especially him, oh indeed, especially him.

These daydreams did not come in the form of reveries when he was sitting lost in thought, when he was alone and still, or at ease. They would be prompted by books or music, by films or plays or songs. If such things stirred him in any way the effect was to send him roaming restlessly through the streets or the roads, his head full of images from whatever it was that had moved him, except that he was also in some way present in those images and being witnessed by her, her father and mother, all her admirers and lovers, the thousand-a-year man well to the fore.

Her beauty was not of the dainty petite kind but was on a more ample scale. There was, as they say, plenty of her. Even alone on the snapshot you could see that she was tall and strapping as well as lovely. It was remarked that she took after her mother who sang a vigorous soprano in the church choir. When her mother had an illness and lost a lot of weight people vied with one another to illustrate how failed she was, such a big strong woman. His father gave some instances demonstrating her strength and showing ruefully that he had cause to know it. There was the business of the Christmas mistletoe in the vestry just after they had performed Handel's *Messiah* in which she had sung so magnificently 'I know that my Redeemer liveth'. His father had kissed a couple of the choirgirls under the mistletoe. A bit of a cod at Christmas. Harmless foolery, you understand. The Rector himself present. All taken in good part by the girls. But when he laid hold of *her* he was damned but she fetched him such a box on the ear it nearly felled him to the ground. His head rung for a day. Oh a big strong woman they all agreed sadly, it would be a while before she could do that again, so badly failed. Then there was the time she nearly fell coming out of the choir pew. The tiles in the aisle had such a polish they were like glass. You would have thought, his father said indignantly, that Mullen the sexton did it on purpose. The feet left her as she stepped out and she made a grab at him to steady herself. Such a grip! God help us all! Blue finger marks up and down his arm for a week! Oh yes, they said, a big strong woman, it's as well we don't know what's in front of us.

He was not sure he liked his father telling the mistletoe story. He would rather his father had told only the choir pew story. It made him uneasy to hear his father speak humorously of kissing the choirgirls, let alone laying hands upon his darling's mother, even for a cod at Christmas with the Rector present. Nor did he like it when they remarked that her daughter took after her, a big strong woman with a bosom and a powerful voice who had given him such a robust hug when she said *this is the one I like*. Her daughter was beautiful and her embrace was softer.

She had a great mass of rich brown hair, and each of the different ways she wore it seemed more becoming then the others; sometimes she piled it high to show her lovely neck, sometimes she tied it with a pretty ribbon, sometimes she let it hang and had to shake it from her eyes with a toss of her head that made him long to gaze at her for hours and hours. He would gaze at the snapshot with the words on the back saying she was just a friend and remember the feel of her long hair when he had run his fingers through it one October evening with a fine clear sky of stars and he had framed her face with her hair, first like this and then like that, and had made it tumble down her face like a veil that he had gently drawn apart to gaze and gaze at and then to kiss.

But that was before. Before he began to doubt. Before he became aware that he might have to compete for her with others. At her seventeenth birthday party the thousand-a-year man stood up and made a speech, nervously at first, then with growing confidence, inserting little self-deprecating jokes that went down well, finally with triumph at having done something manly. Was that what women admired, Joe wondered in dismay. Cold dismay had gripped his heart.

Perhaps if he were to do something famous, memorable, worthy of being pointed out. If he could display some talent that was not commonplace. If only he could sing, tell witty stories, play an instrument, paint pictures, write books. But he had no voice, a poor ear for music, could not do a turn at parties, and, as for writing books, every time he tried there would rise up before him to mock him all the fine books he had read in which what he thought of doing was done infinitely better. Even when he set out merely to study the facts of Irish history for background to a great epic novel he thought he might try his hand at he was daunted to find that the facts themselves seemed far more full of drama than anything he might invent. He sent her a small notebook containing the outline of his novel and waited for her to let him know that she might love him if he wrote it but she returned it without saying that, so he lost heart. His great epic novel was set in Paris and Belfast during the years of revolution and the rebellion of 1798. He browsed in history books in the second-hand bookshops of Smithfield, and, notwithstanding his dismay at the multitude of historical personages who seemed more interesting than the characters he invented, he might still have got a great epic novel onto paper if only she had given him a sign that she would love him if he did.

Sometimes in his daydreams his great epic novel was complete and in some way was not just being read by, but being witnessed by her, and by the fellows at the birthday party, her parents, the thousand-a-year man. It was as if they were actually *seeing* it, with himself both in it as one, or indeed many, of the characters, and yet at the same time visible to one side of it as author, as creator, presenting it like a great spectacle. Every time he came across an episode in the history books that caught his imagination it would turn up in his daydreams about her, woven into his great epic novel, and seen by her and all her admirers.

He had a notebook in which he had jotted down things for his great epic novel: events, places, people, and he would read it sadly for the sake of seeing her face that had inspired it rise before him.

But here and there in its pages were scribblings about other things. These other items were preceded by bizarre doodles indicating that the great epic novel had just then run out of steam and his mind had turned with relief to bits of nonsense. A great scene upon the scaffold, in which a condemned rebel of 1798 was supposed to make a fine seditious speech before dying had petered out in a rash of drawings, stars, faces, monsters, little stick men, and then the rousing words: Up Your Pipe, Your Da Is A Plumber. There were passages that obviously referred to Mr Laffin the jobbing builder whom Joe did the books for, to earn some money in his spare time. Amongst material for his great epic novel Mr Laffin would emerge heralded by a screen of doodles and stick men, or, if not Mr Laffin himself, then the names of things from his trade, which Joe found to be rich in strange and pleasing words: swan-necks, eaves gutters, Bangor blues, hodsman, architrave, U-bends, *Stubbs's Gazette*. His uncle in the Masonic had got him the job. His uncle had taken him to meet Mr Laffin and said, 'Here he is, Alfie, here's a lad will put those books of yours in order and keep you out of *Stubbs's*.' Joe had asked his father what *Stubbs's* was. Busted, Bankrupt, explained Mr McCabe sternly, your name listed in *Stubbs's Gazette*. Carey Street, added Mr McCabe gravely to round the thing off, you'll hear tell of men being in Carey Street. Where the bankruptcy court is in London, and Mr McCabe fell into musing upon bailiffs, sheriff's men, distraint of goods paying two shillings in the pound to creditors, better men than him in *Stubbs's*.

Joe's great epic novel had a scene in London and Carey Street seemed an appropriate setting: all fog, attorneys, prostitutes, hard-up officers on half pay and an eccentric Ulsterman in bed wearing a top hat and bandying sad witty exchanges with saucy serving wenches, but all this ended abruptly in a series of geometric figures with mouths and eyes and then the words in large block capitals: PAY NIGHT BRICKIE BLAMES BAD PINT FOR MORNING AFTER followed by disjointed passages greatly taken up with Mr Laffin's appearance, demeanour and little ways. Unkempt. Swarthy. Blue-black stubble or gun-metal jaws when smooth – the word 'villainous' was scratched out and 'piratical' substituted before 'aspect' – would laugh at a Gillette, a cut-throat or unshaven. 'Shifty-eyed' was scratched out and 'darts little black side-looks at people' substituted. Always girning, whingeing, complaining, querulous. The first two words had question marks at them in case they might not be standard English but Ulster dialect. After 'querulous' he had written 'choleric' but had cancelled it to substitute 'cholerique' instead, the old-fashioned spelling. *Of A Cholerique Humour* he had written and was pleased with the fine historical ring to it. No stranger to the tavern and the bawdy house, his mouth full of oaths and blasphemies, but in mortal fear of hell-fire and damnation. Often repents. A hinge of spittle at the corner of his mouth when vexed. Prays and quakes the morning after with dissenting preachers at their meeting houses and conventicles but breaks out again in drunkenness and lecherie. *Was troubled with the stone and dare not eat anie onion nor grease for fear of agonies with the wind.*

When he read these things over he thought of love. Oh my love, my love, he thought, and he would remember the veil he had made of her hair that fine clear night to make a mystery of her that he could unveil with awe against the shining stars.

Joe and Mr Laffin entered the Ulster Bank at a run just before it closed. People seeing them said to each other that one of these days Alfie Laffin would leave it too late and his men would not get paid. They said this with a laugh, so much was Mr Laffin's last minute dash to the bank a part of the Friday scene, though for Mr Laffin the drawing of the wage cheque was not a laughing matter, especially if he had more than the usual trouble in scraping together something to put in his account, which was always overdrawn.

It seemed to Mr Laffin that Fridays were coming round more and more frequently than before. No sooner over the fret and worry of one than another was upon him. He sometimes gave himself a bad turn in the mornings by thinking it was Friday when it was not. His wife had caused him to come flying down the stairs in his drawers the other morning just by calling up to him, 'Hi Alfie, do you know what day it is?' as he was taking five minutes in bed to mull things over. But she had only meant it was his birthday. 'He's fifty today,' she had told Joe, half-amused at the wonder of it, and in his alarm and relief that it wasn't Friday Mr Laffin had let out a curse for which he had to apologise.

But once inside the portals of the bank, and as always happened on Fridays, his harassed and resentful spirit found a few moments that were almost like peace. The bank was old and solid and spacious. It was as pillared as a house of worship and there was stained glass in the arched windows. Their steps echoed on the marble tiling as if they were in church. Moreover there was always present among the customers one or other of the prosperous businessmen of the locality who would greet Mr Laffin affably and make him feel, for the moment at least, that he was one of their number, that he had indeed joined at last the ranks of the elect, of those whose businesses were well round the corner financially, whose heads were above the water, not worried about a pound or two, able when the occasion called for it to put their hands in their pockets. One of them now affected to be in despair over when his new garage would be started and said that his wife was asking had Alfie Laffin fled the country. Mr Laffin's spirits rose in the ensuing half-serious banter. It did him good to exchange rough pleasantries with moneyed men, and he took no offence at all, when another of the businessmen, in taking his leave, said humorously, 'Well, keep out of *Stubbs's* Alfie', since it gave him the chance to shout back that he'd give ten to one on bigger men than him being in Carey Street before him. The clerks all looked up at the noisy camaraderie that filled the hall. It was the same every Friday when Mr Laffin came rushing in.

Nevertheless this Friday things were a little different for two reasons. One was that, in spite of the outward show of fellowship with the businessmen he met in the bank, the fact remained that since the previous Friday his application to join the Masonic Order had been turned down. Even as he entered into the good-natured teasing about bankruptcy and having the bailiffs in he could not help wondering if it had been one of the men before him who had blocked him in the Mason's secret ballot. The other thing was that there was more delay than usual in cashing his wage cheque. There was always some delay while the cashier went to see if it was all right but this time he had to wait longer and when the cashier returned it was to say that the manager would like a word with him.

The manager first put Mr Laffin at his ease by speaking of the weather. He said that it was hard to tell what kind of a day it was. You could hardly call it rain, he said, referring to the faint drizzle outside, though he added very shrewdly that it would wet you just the same.

Then he got down to business. Mr Laffin's account was in arrears and it was getting progressively more in arrears. Furthermore he had noticed that nearly all the entries in it, both debits and credits, were for round sums. Fifty pounds. Two hundred. Fifty. Fifty. Three hundred. Seventy-five. He hardly ever saw an account like it for such neat figures. What did that mean, he wondered. As if he didn't know. Mr Laffin suddenly saw how revealing the neat figures were and what a fool he had been not to see that they were revealing. Advances on jobs before they were completed, bills never paid in full but only something on account and the rest carried forward. When the manager saw that Mr Laffin knew that he knew what the figures meant he said that he would let them meet the cheque this time but from now on the account would have to be at least in credit on pay days even if he let the wage cheque overdraw it *pro tem*. He would not stop the wage cheque this week because he did not like to see men not getting their pay. There had been one or two cases of that recently and it was something he did not like to see. It was bad for business to see men standing about wondering if they'd get their pay.

143

When the manager let them out into the main hall he spoke again of the baffling indefinability of the weather. That sun, he said, glancing up at the glow behind the stained glass windows, is doing its level best to break through that sky.

Mr Laffin suddenly remembered that the bank manager was a Mason. He wondered aloud to Joe if he was the one who had vetoed him. It took only one black bean dropped into the voting bowl, he told Joe solemnly. He referred to his innocence in the way he gave and received cheques. Could nobody have warned him? Why hadn't somebody tipped him the wink? He darted a little reproachful black side look at Joe.

His van was parked at the kerb and he jumped into it, so obviously sunk in a black study that the men who were in the back shouted to remind him that they were towing a cement-mixer. The men had great misgivings about the safety or even the legality of this operation because the mixer was not being towed on a rope but by themselves gripping the handle. Mr Laffin had been adamant that they could not wait till he got a lorry to transport the mixer properly; the men guessed that this was connected with his need to raise an urgent advance payment on condition that work was seen to start. But even though he drove very slowly at a funereal pace the men were jarred painfully by the clanking mixer; the iron wheels faithfully transmitted every little bump through the rigid iron handle right into their bones.

The slow-moving dark van attracted amused attention. A group of the men's acquaintances were loafing at the door of a public house waiting for the afternoon horse racing to start on the radio in the bar. One of these idlers had the witty idea of doffing his cap and standing very solemn as if a hearse were passing. The others doubled up with laughter and slapped each other on the back. They were so overcome with merriment that they hung onto each other for support. The men in the van responded angrily at first with 'up-you' gestures but then they too laughed a little, though ruefully. One of them, a Catholic called Hagan, shouted that they must be breaking a dozen laws at least and that they'd all get jail if the peelers saw them.

This remark and the loud agreement with which it was endorsed nettled Mr Laffin, chiefly because it was Hagan who said it. He said to Joe that was the thanks he got for giving work to people without fear or favour. Some people wouldn't have Catholics about the place but he had never been a bigot. Now look at the thanks he got for taking Papishes off the dole. Mr Laffin said that Hagan would have to go. If he had to cut his wage bill to sweeten that whore's get of a bank manager then Hagan would be the first. Mr Laffin thought bitterly of the ingratitude of men who could sit at their ease smoking in the back of a van while he was being humiliated trying to get them their money and then complain when he asked them to do a simple thing like moving a cement-mixer to a job.

When they reached the site Mr Laffin found to his annoyance that a man was waiting for him. It was his plasterer McClure, a great giant of a man who could exhaust the strongest labourer, such was the speed with which he could apply plaster, but who had a weakness for drink and went on week-long benders every now and then. He was on one now. He swayed like a tree in the wind as he greeted them vociferously. He was after money for drink. The men marvelled at how he had known where to come. They speculated eagerly on the unseen power that seemed to watch over drunk men, how they could fall without injury, find their way home from strange places, and, as in this instance, be guided by a wonderful instinct.

The men watched appreciatively as Mr Laffin dealt with the figure towering over him. They saw him pull a thick wad of banknotes from his pocket and peel one off. Then as the huge plasterer clasped him round the shoulder in a hug of congratulation Mr Laffin quickly peeled off another pound note. McClure swung round to face the men and his grip was so powerful that he swung Mr Laffin round with him, seeming to be showing him to them.

'This,' he proclaimed in a stentorian voice, 'is a WHITE MAN.'

McClure had been a soldier in India and Africa and he left no-one in doubt that this expression was one of high commendation. Moreover he seemed to be settling once and for all a matter that had been long disputed. He singled out Hagan to repeat this message to and instructed him never to forget that Alfie Laffin was a WHITE MAN. Then he lumbered off the site back to the public houses.

Mr Laffin poked about finding fault as the men unloaded tools and gear and let their aching joints recover from the painful journey. He warned against burning good timber to boil their tea cans. He wanted no complaining about scaffolding – when *he* served his time you had to run up and down ladders and not a penny if you broke your neck! He said that he was far too soft. Being too soft would be his downfall. He spoke the names of other builders in dire tones indicating how very differently the shortcomings of the men would be treated *there*. Ah ha! By Christ! God forgive him for swearing. The thought of how easy-going he was filled Mr Laffin with such a passion that a white hinge of spittle formed at the corners of his mouth. If he wasn't so bloody soft, he declared on almost exactly the same spot on which he had been pronounced a WHITE MAN, he would have made his fortune long ago.

Joe went around collecting the men's time sheets. Some spoke to him seriously about overtime rates and their wicked income tax. Others teased him about women. That woman where they were putting in the damp course. Why didn't he get in there! Fancied him. Filled in her forms for her eh! Never done enquiring about him. Where's my boyfriend, she says, that nice lad. Fancies a bit of spring lamb! She'd put a bit of hair on his chest! What did he mean *old*! A woman in her prime! God those legs! She'd make the smoke come out of his ears! They teased him with these and other expressions of varying coarseness, some drawn from the plumbing end of the building trade which is especially rich in the naming of male and female unions. *Old!* They'd sooner have those legs lapped round them than Hagan's wellingtons! Hagan said he wished he had Joe's chances there! What was holding him? What was he scared of? Here, said Hagan, and took something from his pocket which the others greeted with knowing remarks about the week's supply and not to leave the wife short. He extracted a small object from a packet and placed it in Joe's hand saying it was time he made a start in life. Joe could not conceal his shock and they all laughed when Hagan refused to take it back and Joe uncertainly put it into his wallet. They thought he was shocked by what Hagan had given him and it was true that he had never before seen an unused contraceptive still in its shiny little envelope. But one of the bricklayers was more perceptive. He spoke slyly to Joe out of earshot of Hagan.

'You thought,' the brickie accused softly with a smile, 'you thought the Papishes didn't use the rubber goods.'

He did indeed. He blushed with shame at the imputation of naivety. He sat in the van digesting this new fact of life while Mr Laffin leapt into a trench to solve some problem involving sewer pipes and Joe heard him shouting angrily about the bloody female end and a voice not Mr Laffin's make the suggestion to put a bit of hair round it, they would get it in then all right.

On this note they left the site, Mr Laffin acutely conscious that his handling of the plasterer had been somehow faulty and could have made him look foolish. He knew that the episode would lose nothing in the telling. He sensed that it was being stored in the minds of the men with subtle changes such as that the huge grip in which he had been clasped had not only held him like a child but had lifted him clean off his feet. Then there was the business of hesitating between one of the pound notes and the other. Those with a gift for clowning would make a bar roar with laughter over that. Mr Laffin said to Joe bitterly what a terrible thing money was. Even when you had a wad of it in your pocket you could be made a mockery of because of it. He gave the wad to Joe almost angrily though not before he had peeled off some notes and stuffed into his pocket, affecting not to hear Joe saying 'I need all that Mr Laffin to stamp the men's cards'.

Mr Laffin brooded sombrely all the way back to the yard. The charade at the public house, the interview with the bank manager, the encounter with McClure on a bender, all did nothing to raise his spirits and his wife saw that he was in a black mood when he rushed in to refresh himself with a cup of tea before resuming the struggle. Joe busied himself with the fine calf-bound wages ledger that had been his first administrative reform along with a green filing cabinet in which the bills from Mr Laffin's creditors were stored in alphabetical order, while Mr Laffin sat hunched over the fire holding the cup in both hands. But when he finally spoke, it was his being turned down by the Masons that he chose to be aggrieved about. Let them not think, he told his wife, that he didn't know who had done it. Right bloody well he knew, he cried, who had dropped in the black bean, and he added, God forgive me for swearing, Peggy dear. He always added this when he let out a curse nowadays. He had begun to worship in the Gospel Hall of which his wife had been a devotee for much longer and he had promised her that he would give up swearing just as he had given up the drink. The great victory that he had won, helped by prayer, over the drink, encouraged her to believe that he would one day soon follow her into the fold by going through a ceremony of baptism at the Gospel Hall, accompanied by lusty hymn-singing and testimony-giving, making him, like her, one of the elect who are born again in Christ and assured of salvation.

Mr Laffin said again that he knew who the Judas was who had dropped in the black bean. He gave her very deep and significant looks to let her know that she was to go about saying this though he was careful to name nobody as she was too indiscreet.

'Damned well I know,' he burst out again, and, before he could stop himself, added, 'who dropped in that fucking black bean.'

He saw the look of horror on his wife's face and hastened to do something to make amends.

'God forgive them Peggy dear,' he cried passionately, 'for making me use that awful word.'

Mrs Laffin was a small but spirited woman and their marriage had been stormy and full of shouting matches. She shouted at him now. After giving her his solemn word. Such a mouth he had on him. How could he hear the Gospel with a mouth like that. She burst into tears. He was so conscious of being in the wrong that he sat quiet under her reproaches. She told him that there were no black beans at the foot of the cross. Certainly she could understand him being angry at men not man enough to come out from behind a black bean but when he stood in repentance at the throne of grace there would be no hand *there* to come sneaking in a black bean to keep him out of the Promised Land.

'They don't black-bean you,' she cried, 'at the gates of the Kingdom'.

She left him with that thought at the fire and went to the kitchen, where she fervently sang a hymn. 'Rock of Ages, cleft for me, let me hide myself in Thee'. She often sang hymns as she did her housework. She sang them for all sorts of reasons: to give expression to her new and burning faith; because the words of the hymns appealed to her more directly than the less simple words of the scriptures; because she loved the rousing tunes; because she had a rather sweet voice and loved singing. Now she sang to reproach her husband. One of the verses seemed to fit his case so aptly that she came to the door and sang it at him. 'Foul, I to the fountain fly; Wash me, Saviour, or I die'.

Mr Laffin brooded on awhile at the fire and as he did so the rebuff he had suffered at the hands of the Masons faded. So too did the warning of the bank manager. He had after all spent too many years always on the brink of bankruptcy not to have developed to the full that resilience in his nature which expressed itself in jokes and badinage about *Stubbs's Gazette* and Carey Street. He thought instead of the seemingly trivial incident at the public house when the gambler had doffed his cap in mock reverence of the dead. He now saw it in a more sinister light. The figure on the pavement kept coming before his eyes as literally a mourner at his funeral. He saw it as a token of his death and extinction. It would never have occurred to him to think like that until very recently. But now he was fifty years of age. Of all the many trying events of the recent past the one that after all depressed

him most was the one that seemed so unimportant at
the time: his fiftieth birthday. He suddenly realised that
his death was no longer remote. Three score and ten was
the allotted span. Only twenty years left. It was no use
all his contemporaries telling each other that fifty was
not old, citing instance after instance of people making
new starts at fifty, marrying at fifty, emigrating at fifty.
Fifty was no age *these* days they said. Look at Churchill.
Look at Bernard Shaw. But what fifty was, Mr Laffin kept
thinking, was only twenty years from seventy and the play-
acting at the public house brought his coffin clearly before
his mind's eye. Anger flared up in him again at how his
men in the van had laughed and the laughter he remembered
most was Hagan's. He thought again of the man's
ingratitude at not having it held against him that he was
a Catholic.

'That Hagan fella,' he said to Joe, 'did you hear him
insulting me at Mercer's Bar?'

He shouted for another cup of tea and as he drank it
he thought of McClure the plasterer and of the destination
of those two pound notes. He felt envious. He pictured
the dark foaming stout in the glass and remembered the
sour smooth taste. He recalled the tingling warmth that
would spread itself gently over the brain. He thought with
longing and regret of the tolerance, affection, love even,
into which that warmth would sometimes translate itself
and be marvellously sustained for hour after hour. Mr
Laffin remembered the love that had flowed out of him
to all around him on such occasions and had filled his
soul with joy. His soul had insisted on being kept filled
to the brim with love for his fellow men until his money
had run out. Even now when the prayers of his wife had
been answered and he never touched a drop he secretly
looked back on certain of those days when he had been
filled with love from morning till night as the most exalted

of his life and almost worth all the other days of drinking when he had pursued that state of exaltation in vain and with dreadful sickness. When the preachers in the Gospel Hall spoke of the love of God that passeth all understanding he sometimes was tempted to compare it with those days of exaltation. As the recollection of them came back to him he shifted his hold upon the tea cup until he was gripping it as if it were a glass.

After he had gone Mrs Laffin began looking forward to Sunday. She loved Sunday. Her Alfie was so different on Sundays. So relaxed. Sunday really was a day of rest for him. Six days shalt thou labour and, do all thy work. On Sundays Mr Moreton of the Gospel Hall came round with some other Christians and her Alfie sat at his ease among them in the parlour, so beautifully furnished in all the latest styles from the household departments of the builders' merchants where her Alfie had his accounts. Mrs Laffin often ordered things on Mr Laffin's accounts. China cabinets; fireside companion sets; poufs, a picture of the Stag At Bay. It was true that the Stag At Bay had caused a shouting match. Hi Peggy, what bloody stag at bay, he had come running in shouting. He had waved invoices at her and cursed, and she had shouted back at him that she had told him about it if only he would listen, that the Stag At Bay had been up there looking at him for a week!

But on Sundays the parlour shone with Christian feeling and optimism. It was then that Mr Laffin indulged himself with the luxury of optimism both about his business affairs and the fate of his eternal soul. This optimism had shone especially bright the previous Sunday. Mr Moreton had offered prayers for the acceptance by Mr Laffin of Christ crucified, which had been joined in by several other prominent men from the Gospel Hall, men who were not only brothers in the Lord but prosperous in business too, and their line of large cars along the street had attracted many an envious glance. Theirs was a state of grace, which, it seemed to Mr Laffin, included also being well round the corner financially, and whereas on weekdays this sometimes made him resentful, it was different on Sundays, above all on the previous Sunday when he had felt so near to a state of grace himself that he had been imbued with a warm sense of fellowship. As they had risen from their knees after praying for his salvation, so strongly had this feeling taken possession of him that he had, as it were, almost appointed himself their spokesman in explaining to some of his relatives present who were humble wage-earners what a very different way of life it was if you were a man of business. All done by cheques and accounts, said Mr Laffin expansively. Hardly ever saw the colour of money except to pay the men. Cheques every place. Wasn't that so, Mr Laffin appealed to Mr Moreton. Wasn't it, he appealed to the men from the Gospel Hall. Mrs Laffin, bustling in with the cakes, was delighted at the sight of her husband seeming already to be what she prayed for him to become. She responded to the happy scene by making the gesture children make when they are touched – for she was small in person and somewhat childlike in her emotions – of putting her head to one side and almost saying 'ah'.

Next Sunday would be even better. She felt that her husband was nearly ready to be converted. Mr Moreton was bringing round Mr Wallace who had done so well in his handkerchief factory. What did her Alfie want to bother with the old Masonic for, she thought indignantly.

Joe had nearly finished the wage packets when Sandra Laffin, the daughter, came home from the mill where she was a secretary. She was full of talk of the victories she had scored against the secretaries of other men less well served. She was a bold handsome girl progressing daily in the stern task she had set herself of acquiring the mannerisms and turns of speech of the better class of people in the suburbs to which she aspired. She had a mass of dark hair and her white skin was marked by downiness especially round her mouth which Joe often dreamt of smothering in kisses. She often teased him about his alleged romances. She was a year older than he and consequently felt entitled to adopt the manner of a woman of the world amused at young love. But today Sandra asked indignantly if her Daddy had not stamped those cards yet. Oh Mummy he is awful, she complained. After the trouble she took to read out to him cases in the papers of employers had up for not stamping their men's cards. She asked Joe to let her see how far behind the cards were. She leaned over him and enveloped him with her hair, her red mouth, her girl smell. She gave little shrieks at what she saw. Her Daddy really was the limit.

Mr Laffin's yard was at the back of the house and the sitting room commanded a view of it. By the time his van drove into it for the last time that Friday, a number of people both in the house and in the yard were awaiting his arrival. Men were gathered in the yard waiting for their pay. They included the cement-mixer towing party who were demonstrating the strains they had suffered in various limbs and the risks they had been made to run. Hagan took off his cap slowly and solemnly like the wag at the public house and they all laughed. Then, having a talent for that kind of thing, he re-enacted the episode with the drunken plasterer, clasped the small bricklayer round the shoulders so as to lift him clean off the ground before switching roles and miming the peeling off of banknotes while being swung in the air, at which the men

154

roared so merrily that the people in the sitting room looked out but could make nothing of it.

Mr Moreton of the Gospel Hall was one of those who looked out. He had come to sound out the prospects of a decisive step by Mr Laffin towards becoming a brother in Christ and also to bring his account, for it was a fact that one or two of the neat round figures in Mr Laffin's bank account were payments to Mr Moreton. Mr Moreton was not only a notable bearer of witness for the Lord Jesus but a very successful trader in women's garments who took whole pages in the local paper to proclaim the message of the latest styles.

Mr Laffin rushed into the sitting room. He had seen Hagan's pantomime out of the corner of his eye and he darted a little black side-look at Mr Moreton for having seen it too.

'I'm paying Hagan off,' he said to Joe. 'Give me his cards.'

'I have no Insurance stamps, Mr Laffin,' said Joe. 'I can't stamp his cards. We can't pay him off this week.'

Mr Laffin nearly let out that awful word. Only Mr Moreton's presence made him check it in time. Why hadn't Joe said earlier, he demanded furiously. How could *he* think of everything with so much on his mind. He would have to consider getting somebody else to do the books who could take these burdens off him.

But both Sandra and Mrs Laffin came to Joe's defence. Mrs Laffin made it clear that if her husband took that line with Joe there would be a shouting match whether Mr Moreton was there or not. Mr Laffin quickly changed his tune and he suggested a way out of the difficulty. He hunted through the pile of National Insurance cards which Sandra had been so scathing about and extracted one with a cry of triumph. It was that of a man who had been with Mr Laffin for only a week and which was therefore almost fully stamped. He picked with his thumbnail at one of the stamps and called to his wife to put the kettle on.

'You could steam them off that one,' he said to Joe in a conniving wheedling tone, 'and stick them on Hagan's.'

'No,' said Sandra in a hard voice. She snatched the card from her father's hand and placed herself between him and Joe. 'No,' she said again, very loudly and sharply.

'My father,' she began to explain harshly and contemptuously in the blunt accents of the streets around them before correcting herself, 'my Daddy,' she began again, smilingly as if her father's little foibles were not to be taken seriously, 'my Daddy will get us all jail, so he will.'

Mr Laffin acknowledged the superiority of the forces opposing him and rushed out to the yard with the wage packets. Sandra said, lady-like and amused, that it was like feeding time at the Zoo out there. Joe was so flustered by lovely Sandra, so magnificent in her scorn, that all he could think about wages was that the *wages of sin is death*, or rather he thought that Mr Moreton must be thinking that as he stood looking out at the Friday night pay scene in the yard, for Joe found it impossible to think of Mr Moreton's mind as containing anything but words of holy scripture.

Mrs Laffin was looking out at it too. It was a scene that always touched Mrs Laffin with feelings of anger, pity and pride. Her Alfie seemed so beleaguered and at bay with all those thankless hands reaching out at him. Sometimes it seemed to her that he was actually warding off blows, and the blows seemed to be aimed not only at him but at her too. Her Alfie seemed to be fighting off a world that would engulf them both and surely the Lord Jesus was at his side in the struggle. She would have liked to have put that thought into words and to have expressed it to Mr Moreton, for he had been her mentor at the time of her own conversion and she valued his approbation. But the only words she could think of were those of one of the Gospel hymns that she was so fond of. *Onward, upward, till victorious, Thou shalt lay thine armour down, And thy loving Saviour bids thee, At His hand receive thy crown.* She did not like quoting hymns to Mr Moreton as freely as she would to her husband or her friends because she knew that Mr Moreton did not entirely approve of her inclination to regard the lines of hymns as if they were themselves sacred words of scripture like the texts which came so readily to his own lips to support his cooler brand of evangelising. She ventured to say that she was sure Alfie was nearly ready to be saved and Mr Moreton agreed that Mr Laffin was daily drawing nigh onto Zion.

Mr Moreton said that quite sincerely. He firmly believed that Mr Laffin's baptism in Christ crucified was indeed imminent and he was vain enough to want the credit for it, for Mr Moreton's favourite text was one he rarely quoted since he had taken it so much onto himself. 'I will make you fishers of men.' Mr Moreton's well-dressed figure was often seen standing in the warmly-lit vestibule of the Gospel Hall, his hands folded complacently over the groin, gazing serenely out onto what he so obviously thought of as the Broad Highway of Life on which people heedlessly passed by, going in and out of public houses, the cinema, Genesi's fish and chip shop, careless of the peril to their immortal souls.

'Yes,' said Mr Moreton confidently, 'Mr Laffin is half way across the Jordan.'

He managed to slip the envelope containing his account to Joe who was not quite sure what to do with it. Then he took his leave.

'Mr Laffin,' he assured Mrs Laffin, 'is within sight of the Kingdom.'

Mrs Laffin continued to gaze out of the window at her

husband paying the men, not without disputes in which voices were raised. Although in some ways a rather naive little person she could have added to the places on Mr Moreton's Broad Highway that stood as symbols for the sinful pleasures of the world a place that would not have occurred to him, and moreover a darker place by far than any of his, one in which her Alfie had not only fought the good fight and won but in which he had demonstrated his love for her too. She knew of it only from overhearing a group of the men talking without knowing that she was near. The men had been discussing, with a foul language that had made her ears burn, a subject even more shocking than their language, for it was nothing else than the secret brothels of Belfast or 'bad houses' as the men called them. It appeared that Mr Laffin and a party of drinking cronies had found themselves in a 'bad house' situated mysteriously off the Lisburn Road, but he had been too far gone in drink to realize immediately where he was. It was only when a woman came and sat on his knee that, in the words of the men, he had twigged it where they were. He had rushed out of the place crying, 'I love my Peggy, I love my Peggy,' and the other men had to rush out too in case of trouble. The men listening to this story had joined in at the part where Mr Laffin had called out his wife's name, recognising a situation in which his plaintive tones would have been conspicuous. They had chorused, 'I love my Peggy, I love my Peggy,' in mocking derision and Mrs Laffin had crept away appalled and yet also proud.

In moments when she was cast down and discouraged, such as when she realized that they had a daughter who was ashamed of them, she would remember that dreadful story and be comforted. She was one of those little women who carry over from childhood not only a smallness of person which itself had something still childlike about it but also the feeling that things would always be a bit too big for them. In spite of her quick temper and her ability to give as good as she got in shouting matches with her husband, she often felt bewildered by life, swept along, frightened. But when she thought of her Alfie not only defying Satan in that 'bad house' but proclaiming his love for her even with the drink in him, her feet, as it were, touched rock. *Rock of Ages, cleft for me, let me hide myself in Thee.*

She put her head on one side to admire him in the yard, where, surrounded by disgruntled men, he seemed to be the very rock on which her life was built.

A child put its head round the door offering to run an errand to the shops, and Mrs Laffin reached for her purse. There was not enough in it, so she helped herself to some money from what was left of the wages, money Joe had been hoping to put aside towards stamping the men's cards. She asked him sweetly had he had his money yet. He had. He was just putting it into his wallet where a small ominous bulge threatened to long reproach him with his unloseable virginity.

'Away up to Genesi's,' Mrs Laffin said fondly to the child, 'and get a fish and chip for Mr Laffin's tea.'

14

'Belfast is not a city of miracles. The waters of its river are not bottled by the enterprising for sale to the devout nor do pilgrims kneel at famous shrines. This is not because of any lack of reports of happenings, visions, visitations, cures when hope was gone, but because the prevailing mentality, though credulous, is truculent, and lacks that uniformity of outlook by which a ripple of amazement can continue to spread without loss of energy across the junction of men's minds.'

Joe was pleased with having written that himself, so much did it look like something copied from a book. He got it typed, explaining that it was something copied from a book, and the fact that this explanation was accepted without question confirmed his pride in having written something very fine. He pasted the typed page into the large leather-bound notebook in which he was making a fresh start after destroying the ones which contained the notes for his great epic novel. He could no longer bear to read it, since it seemed only to contain a portrait of himself as a failed lover.

His new notebook was really very old. He had found it after he went to work in Taylor's Mill, covered in dust that had preserved its newness. It was in fact an old spinning room order book for the year 1886, just started and then abandoned, leaving all those unused pages bound in leather, seeming to cry out for the pen. He had found it at the back of the old yarn store along with a tin plate advertisement for linen threads, of the kind that used to be common at railway stations, except that this one was in Spanish and had a picture of a woman sewing, in a dress down to her ankles. The few used pages of the spinning room order book were filled with beautiful spidery writing of some clerk long dead. Had he died just after starting it? In tragic circumstances? Had they put the ledger aside from superstitious uneasiness? He could well imagine people citing to each other in awe the fact that he had only ruled the first two pages of No. 6 Spinning Room Order Book as evidence of how unforeseen death was, of how none is promised tomorrow.

He had found the tin plate advertisement first and had brought others to see it and to marvel at something so old being at the same time shining new. It gleamed like an icon in the shafts of dusty sunlight streaming through the small windows in the stone walls. There was an address on it. Calle de la Concepcion Inmaculata, Buenos Aires. Street of the immaculate conception. The fellows he showed it to speculated eagerly on the differences between Irish Catholic culture and that of the Spanish-speaking peoples in the matter of what was proper in the way of names. No Irish street could have such a name. Why was that, they wondered. Would have to ask a Catholic, they said. But how could you ask a Catholic a thing like that, they said, when they're not allowed to think about such things. And what about the name of the firm. Jesus Romero y Hijos Limitada. Imagine an Irishman called Jesus! Jesus O'Rourke! O'Jesus no! But of the preserved newness of the tin plate advertisement, of its new oldness or its old newness he could elicit no response of wonder like his own.

He kept the 1886 spinning room order book to himself. The paper of the new/old, old/new foolscap book was thick and creamy. It had a fine glaze to it. The observation about the glaze was not his own. It was Mr Baker's. Mr

Baker was the oldest of the clerks and had beautiful handwriting, rather like that of the long dead clerk in Joe's book, sadly no longer fashionable like some other obsolete office practices which Mr Baker vainly sought to preserve, such as the old method of making corrections in ledgers and order books. Mr Baker deplored the modern habit of bleaching out mistakes with bleach from the dyehouse. All the clerks and typists had their little bottles of bleach which Mr Baker said made ugly marks on fine paper. When a new junior started Mr Baker would attempt to imbue him with the ways of the past. Joe had stood at the side of Mr Baker's desk to watch the Baker method of making corrections. Mr Baker's fingers were dark brown from cigarettes and although smoking was strictly forbidden there always arose from his person the odour of tobacco, some of it unmistakably fresh. His bald head too was very brown, from playing tennis on the mill courts, and huge chocolate-coloured freckles speckled the tight parchment over his skull as if a tea pot had been emptied over him. Were they what people called grave spots, Joe wondered.

Good paper, explained Mr Baker, has a fine glaze to it. Mr Baker produced the little bone handled knife, very sharp, with which he deliberately scraped the fine glaze of the thick creamy paper of a spinning room order book in which there was an error. Scrape, scrape went Mr Baker's knife and a little heap of fibrous dust, part inky-blue, part white glaze steadily accumulated. When all trace of the error had gone Mr Baker would blow away the little heap of dust very deliberately, bending his face towards the paper and rounding his mouth in an O as if to take the scrapings by surprise, giving a sudden whuff from inflated cheeks as though it was essential for them to vanish in an instant. He would again refer to the fine glaze of good paper, which, he explained, would let you polish it again and he showed Joe the old nicotine-stained finger nail, split and cracked, that he used for the purpose. All it needs, he told Joe in a loud confidential whisper meant to be overheard, and pressing his arm in friendly conspiracy, is what people don't have a lot of these days. PATIENCE. There, he said to Joe, go thou and sin no more, and to conclude the demonstration even more finally might rise from his desk and march briskly out of the office with an imposing file under his arm, very spry for his years in his mill tennis club blazer.

Old Baker, some of the other clerks said with scornful laughs, is off to the bog for another smoke. What, asked one of the younger ones does he do with that file? Parks it at the side of the throne, he was told indignantly. It would make you wonder, they said, what you were touching when you go round his desk. Never, they told Joe sternly, as if it was an important part of his office training, never put your hands near your mouth when that man gives you papers.

Beol. A ford. *Fearsad.* A sandbank. BELFAST. He wrote these words in large letters in his 1886 spinning room book. He toyed with the idea of making the B of *Beol* into a huge illuminated mediaeval letter like the monks did to start off the chapters of their famous books. But then he grew very stern with himself for having such childish whims. No More Whims he wrote in a deliberately brutal script. His whims were getting him into trouble, even with the police when he persisted, despite sensible advice, in equipping his new Raleigh cycle with his grandfather's old acetylene lamp and it kept going out due to trouble in the waterworks. Nothing but Truth and Beauty, he wrote. The decline of the mills and the shipyards that had once made Belfast world-famous was a sad truth, and sadness and beauty are closely related. But notwithstanding his wish to put down some beautiful truth about the mills of Belfast, and where more appropriate than the 1886 spinning room book, the first thing he wrote there in the truth and beauty line was about the shipyard even though he had seen no more of the shipyard than could be seen from the tops of buses crossing the Queen's Bridge. Another whim, he told himself resignedly, but went ahead just the same. THE TITANIC, he wrote, going straight for the big one, no messing about with local homespun trifles, and then remembering suddenly something about the *Titanic* from his childhood and writing it down just as it came.

A man on our street was thin and small
And yet was a shipyard blacksmith withal.
He rolled home drunk every Saturday night,
And in a chair in the parlour was propped upright
To be sick on the oilcloth and sober up
Under the picture of the *Titanic*,
Which he had worked on when he was young.
When my toy steamboat blew its whistle off,
He got the shipyard to fix it on again
Once more to sail the bath as good as new.
I remember him only one time more
Laid out in his small coffin
Under the picture of the *Titanic*,
And in the next room in the eager talk
Of re-united friends who would forget each other again
After the funeral ham tea,
He was already being forgotten.
Yet still I recall him drawing up my toy
From the deep pocket of a coat that was too big for
    him
And how I marvelled where,
Amid the crash and roar of tools that had forged
    the *Titanic*
He had found such exquisite delicacy.

The father of the girl he would for ever love worked in the shipyard. Should he polish up 'The *Titanic*' and send it to her, making it rhyme properly, maybe 'sick' with '*Titanic*', and then again maybe not? Would that restore him to her grace? Her father had been a great Union man, sometimes out on strike against the boilermakers, seemingly the deadly rivals of his trade. He spoke vehemently of one of their encroachments and said by God it would be the rock the boilermakers would perish on.

The 1886 book was labelled 'No. 6 Spinning Room'. No. 6 was now the last of the old wet-spinning rooms, warm and steamy, some of the women still in bare feet as of old, and its current order book was easy to spot among the others from being stained with handling by damp hands.

The girls of No. 6 were notorious for bringing a blush to the cheeks of youths passing through by calling out things, making kissing sounds and other amatory noises. Yet although the chorus of cheeping and whistling that came from behind the spinning frames was something of an ordeal for youths not easy in their dealings with girls, there was in it an element of reassurance, even pleasure. Joe sometimes made a journey that was not strictly necessary through No. 6, steeling himself for the ordeal of being whistled and called at, which yet had in it something that was a balm for the precarious self-esteem of a failed lover. One anonymous hussy even managed to imitate with startling accuracy above the roar of the spinning frames that special groaning sound that some men make softly to each other to indicate the discomfort of their virility when a pretty woman passes and which Joe had thought was a code known only to men.

Once a bold handsome girl planted herself right in front of him barring his path and studied him insolently

and coolly. Her beautiful dark eyes had whites like milk
and put his brain in a whirl. His brain whirled along with
the whirling bobbins all round her and an older woman
had to come and rescue him, saying sharply, ah for Jesus
sake Lily have some sense and stop torturing that young
fella like that. Could she really have said that in his ear,
he wondered, a thing like that, a dirty thing like that, a
lovely dirty thing like that. She never blocked his path
again. What opportunity had he been too paralysed to
take? What had he let pass him by? He preserved with
fastidious care the memory of her dark eyes with the
whites like milk and of the dark down fringing her lips
to add to his store of images of allure upon which he
drew in those acts of solitary lust of which he was so
ashamed and which came between him and his intention
to write something fine about the mill-women of Belfast
in his 1886 leather-bound book, which he kept secretly
just where he found it at the back of the old yarn store.

Once someone had come into the store while he was
with it and he had gone motionless as the footsteps
approached, echoing on the wooden floor with planks as
thick as railway sleepers. Underneath was a black void,
and if a stone was dropped through the trapdoor there
would be a pause and then a plop. He had waited with
a beating heart as the footsteps stopped and then to his
relief the figure, outlined in the shafts of sunlight in
which the dust motes danced unceasingly, turned and
went away again. It was while he had been writing something
in the book about the dark-eyed tormentor of No. 6
spinning room. Or perhaps it was another girl she had
put him in mind of.

He had not meant to write about girls at all but about
Sir Malcolm the chairman of the mill and his awful red
eye. Sir Malcolm's terrible eye of blood had suddenly
glowed in the manager's office, where, finding it empty,

Joe had slid cautiously into the high leather chair behind the desk, trying to feel what it was like to be a man of power, when there was this awful buzzing noise from a little box with a speaker on it and a red eye on the box had glared at him balefully and seemed to pursue him buzzing and glaring as he fled. What made him panic, though he laughed later, was that the manager's desk was cluttered with hanks of combed flax just like the hair of fair women which he was reaching out involuntarily to stroke when the red eye came on and caught him at it. He had it in mind to compose something very fine about Sir Malcolm's eye of blood flashing ferociously from the platforms upon the Orangemen on the Twelfth of July, for Joe had once heard Sir Malcolm speak at a Twelfth Field about defending our proud Protestant heritage against the menace of Popery, while bowler-hatted Orangemen pissed along a hedge holding a bottle of stout in their free hand, a few with faces turned towards the platform. But the only thing that came to him in that vein was about an Orange bonfire in which an effigy of Lundy the traitor was burnt ritually and where he had first been kissed by a girl whom he had not known till then was beautiful, when it was too late. So he wrote nothing of the red-eyed gods of hate and war but instead entered the following: 'She kissed me round an Orange bonfire/ In the merry month of sweet July/ Kissed me, teased me, mocked me, spurned me/ Made me lovesick, lovelorn I/ Oh what care I for your bold King Billy/ For your drums and banners nought care I/ But oh for the true-blue girl that kissed me/ In the merry month of sweet July'.

The bowler-hatted foremen of Belfast and the shawled millwomen, he wrote. Their day is over. But the phrases were not his. His uncle in the Masonic had used them when he found Joe what he called an opening in Taylor's Mill after Joe refused adamantly to go to university. The mills these days, his uncle said, need young fellows with a bit of education behind him. Adapt or die, his uncle said that he had said to the man he knew at the mill with a bit of pull, and repeated the phrase several times with satisfaction. Mr McCabe, excited at the speculative turn the talk was taking, would have liked to harangue them on a favourite theme of his, namely the dead hand of old fogeyism in church and state, and was not altogether pleased when one of the others told what in another context was one of Mr McCabe's favourite jokes, the one about the candle that nobody could get their mouths near enough to blow out till the schoolmaster snuffed it out with finger and thumb wetted by licking: that's what a bit of education does for you! Of course, his uncle said sternly, he'll have to take the CERTificates in textiles. Will be allowed time off for it the man said. Just like us, his aunt and a neighbour woman said. What? Yes, maintained the women defiantly, they were part-timers in the mill. Thirteen years of age. One day at school, one in the mill. Used to be such a rush to get through the mill gates before the horn stopped blowing. The man would shut it in your face and you were locked out. But this female contribution was waved aside as an irrelevance. The age of the bowler hat and the shawl is over, said his uncle in the Masonic. Brute force and ignorance, cried Mr McCabe, has had its day.

Thus backed by the forces of freemasonry did youth with a bit of education behind it come to the aid of the once mighty but now ailing linen industry. Every morning Joe rode his bicycle through the huge gate hung on well-oiled rollers to facilitate closing it in the face of shawled mill-girls when the horn stopped, his new Raleigh cycle, with the old acetylene lamp that only needed something poked up its water pipe to save him from the police and the courts, swerving with great panache into the old yarn store, his tyres drumming on the ancient planks of the floor and stopping abruptly a hair's breadth from the stone wall near the place where his book had lain since 1886.

He always rode over the great weigh-bridge for lorries just inside the gate. He liked the tremor beneath him as he rode across the huge iron panel. It appealed to him that something so massive should at the same time be so delicate and sensitive. He liked the notion, conveyed by that faint tremor, of great levers shifting and adjusting about their massive fulcrum in order to maintain their harmony, sensing a faint disturbance to their perfect equilibrium in even so slight a presence as himself.

It was Friday afternoon. It was the last Friday afternoon of its kind that there would ever be. There was to be no more Saturday half-day working. The five-day week had come to the mill. It was the end of an era.

Joe sat at the window in a reverie looking across the cobblestoned mill yard to the old main office, still called 'The Counting House' from long habit, with the date 1783 above its classical portals. The time of the French Revolution and the first mill steam-engine in Belfast. The fall of the Bourbons and the rise of the bowler-hatted foremen. Was it true what the fellows at the canteen table said of the shipyard foremen when work was slack? If a man had a good-looking wife...? Bowler-hatted Belfast foremen exercising *Droit de Seigneur* among the shawled mill-women? Well, it was all over now. There was a five-day week now.

Mr Baker was very much in an end-of-era mood as he rang round his cronies in the mill tennis club and wondered what they would all do with themselves now on a Saturday morning to keep from under the wife's feet. Mr Baker had secured a copy of the document setting it all out and he read from it very solemnly several times.

169

'Employers' Association in agreement with the Trades Unions ... so affording free Saturdays ... time and piece rates advanced ... no monetary loss to workers ... also to apply to office staff.'

Mr Baker passed on admiringly what one of the directors was reputed to have said about the five-day week. Mr John said he wished *he* could have a five-day week. *Young* Mr John. Not old Mr John. Said he wished *he* could belong to a trade union! Mr Baker and the older clerks always referred to the directors by their first names. Sir Malcolm. Mr Henry. Old Mr John. Mr Archibald. The rueful saying of young Mr John that he wished he could join a trade union circulated admiringly among the older clerks as evidence of the great social changes taking place all around them, not all of them, be it said, for the better, though some of the rabble that will neither work nor want would shoot you for saying that.

When Mr Baker was on the telephone he was a very good listener and would only interrupt the other party to contribute brief summings-up of the subject matter in the form of pithy quotations drawn from literature and the scriptures. These, being sometimes entirely separated from what was being said at the other end of the line, seemed to hang free in the air like riddles to guess the meaning of.

'Whence all but he had fled.'

'Some fell upon stony ground.'

'Fools rush in where angels fear to tread.'

'Hanging up his spurs.'

'Converted on the road to Damascus.'

'Change and decay in all around I see.'

The end-of-era mood however had not affected all. From a desk near Joe's came a strange rhythmic murmuring as of someone at prayer. It was Harry. Harry's head was bowed over his desk. Joe watched him absently as the soft chanting continued for a little while then stopped as Harry jumped up and came to Joe's side, holding open a book which he thrust into Joe's hands, rapping peremptorily with his finger at the place on the page that Joe was to look at. Harry had failed the Matriculation at school and was having to sit it again under threats from his family vague but dire. He frowned in concentration and began reciting sternly.

> In Xanadu did Kubla Khan
> A stately pleasure dome decree:
> Where Alph, the sacred river, ran
> Through caverns measureless to man
> Down to a sunless sea.

No Harry, said Joe after a time, no.
What, said Harry angrily, what?
He glared at Joe and snatched back the poetry book, then, seeing his mistake for himself, struck himself on the head quite sharply several times saying damn, damn, damn, damn. He slumped into his chair with his legs sticking straight out and his chin lolling on his chest prostrate with despair, from which attitude he slowly roused himself with an enormous show of effort and began muttering furiously over and over again: A damsel with a dulcimer, In a vision once I saw, A damsel with a dulcimer, In a vision once I saw...

Perhaps prompted by Harry's chanting and memorising and Mr Baker's literary allusions summing up the unknown words of distant speakers, the other clerks began reciting half-humorously poems they had learnt at school and elsewhere.

Not a drum was heard, not a funeral note. To pee or not to pee that is the question. Twas Christmas Day in the workhouse. This sceptred Isle, this Mars amid the sea.

171

Don't go down in the mine Dad, there's plenty of coal in the yard. Who touches a hair of yon grey head. All I ask is a tall ship and the stars to sail her by.

But the medley of quotations subsided and finally died out in favour of one, which to their surprise they all listened to seriously. It was spoken by a thick-set clerk whom nobody would have thought to have a line of poetry in him but he recited some verses in a child's plain solemn way that so obviously came straight from his childhood without the slightest effort of recollection that it made them all stop and think of their own childhoods.

On Lough Neagh's bank as the fisherman strays,
When the clear cold eve's declining,
He sees the round towers of other days
In the wave beneath him shining;
Thus shall memory often, in dreams sublime,
Catch a glimpse of the days that are over;
Thus, sighing, look through the waves of time
For the long faded glories they cover.

A bulbous-nosed man cradling an electric calculating machine in his arms like a child stopped to listen and remarked that it was wonderful how they managed it. Who managed what? The rhymes, he said sternly, the rhymes. How those poet fellows thought of them he would never know. The only time he tried it it nearly killed him, he said ruefully and laid down the adding machine very tenderly when he saw that he would have to explain himself. It was for a death notice in the paper and the wife wanted a wee verse, you know the sort of thing, he said. They did indeed. They read them every evening or had them read out to them by their wives. It was for the old uncle, he said. He personally, he said would have settled for The Lord is My Shepherd or Where No Shadows

Fall. Mr Baker said very firmly that he could never see the need for anything more but the others demurred and the red-nosed clerk said that the wife would hear of nothing else after she saw the one they had made up round at the sister's so there was damn all for it but to rack his brains. But he got there in the end, and not without pride he now spoke the lines he had composed. 'His chair by the fire is empty, But his pipe is still on the rack. For the message has not yet sunk in, That Uncle Bert will never be back.' When his listeners murmured that it was very nice he accepted the compliment modestly but protested again that he would sooner paper two rooms for her than take on a job like that again.

Joe heard the last line of the death notice verse with relief. For some reason he had expected it to go differently – 'Uncle Bert has gone off with a cherubim' – and had been steeling himself for it so that he was almost grateful when it did not. Idly he tried to think of other reminders of a departed presence. Caps still on hall stands. Unwalked dogs. But the red drinker's nose of the do-it-yourself maker of verse kept suggesting other things like empty bar-stools, unchalked billiard cues, unthrown darts, unbacked winners. Stool at the bar now empty, his darts are still on the board. Sadly missed by all the bookies' runners.

But then he felt ashamed of his derision. The clerk, who was always known by his two first names, Sammy John, was a kindly man who had done Joe no harm and indeed had helped him settle in when he first started and was somewhat intimidated by a place full of hard men, roaring machinery and bold tormenting girls. He was almost inclined to show Sammy John a trick or two in the making of verse should the need again arise. He could have helped Sammy John and the wife the night they wrestled – poetically speaking – with Uncle Bert. Make your lists, he would have told them. Lists of words that rhyme with certain words in your first ideas. Like years, tears, fears. Heart, part. You, through, knew, true. Then you shuffle your lines about to get the right word at the end. All the poets did it, he would have assured them, though they wouldn't thank you for broadcasting that about. There was even a rhyming dictionary you could buy if you had the nerve to ask for it in the bookshops. He would bet there were a few well thumbed copies about if you knew where to look. Not prominently on display though. Probably sent by post in plain wrapper and kept at the back of famous poets' desks along with their elastic bands and stomach powders. All I ask is a tall ship. Sip, grip, hip. And a star to sail her by. Lie, nigh, thigh.

Oh yes, he would have assured Sammy John and the wife, there was a lot of that went on all right. He knew the feeling well. It came over him every time he tried to make up a few more verses about the Belfast mills. Rills, hills. He had greatly fancied *rills*. It was one of those poetical words not used in ordinary language. A stream, a small river, a brook. *By cool Siloam's shady rill.* When the sweated mill children of Lancashire asked if they could sing to lighten their labours the owners said yes as long as it was hymns. The mills of Belfast had all been cotton mills once. People didn't seem to know that and when you told them they seemed to wish you hadn't. Belfast changed from cotton to linen after the Napoleonic wars. Not a drum was heard, not a funeral note. Mills, rills. It was the contrast made him fancy *rills* at first, even its artificial poetical flavour heightening the contrast between the lovely land and the red-brick mills, the dingy streets, the gospel halls. But it was too English and he had settled for *hills*. Yet he had little enough to show for it. The subject had proved as intractable as Uncle Bert, notwithstanding ample opportunities to rhyme its rich tapestry of ingredients. Shawls, gospel halls. Loom, doom.

Bleachers, preachers, Doffers, scoffers. Weavers, believers. Spinners, sinners. All he had was one small verse he did not like well enough to copy into his 1886 book since it resisted all his efforts to add to it or prise it open and swell it out. It seemed to have rolled itself up into a tiny pretentious solemn little ball. 'The Truculent Citizens Of Black Belfast', he had got as a heading, a fair enough start, indeed an imposing one. But then only the one little verse, hardly worth its while, God help it. 'They did not dwell by burn nor glen/ Where crystal streams gush down the hills/ But where all about was made by men/ And men were roused not by the rising of the sun/ But by the hooting of the mills.'

Belfast College of Technology shone like a beacon of truth and learning in the early darkness of a misty autumn afternoon, every window ablaze with light as its eager students measured, weighed, calibrated, re-affirmed afresh the great laws that govern the universe in all their principles, coefficients, densities, wavelengths. They did so moreover on an admirably non-sectarian basis. The groups that gathered round Bunsen burners, Wheatstone bridges, refracting prisms, internal combustion engines, or, as in the Flax Spinning class, their spinning frames wet and dry, were composed of both religious persuasions communicating with perfect freedom. And why not? The pure and applied sciences are not usually the areas of Belfast life where the young have had to learn very early to tread warily in what is called 'mixed company'.

When the bell went for break and everybody rushed to the canteen, the little group from Flax Spinning included a couple of Catholics, but good fellows nonetheless, highly esteemed for their jokes, their racy stories about rugby parties, dance halls, drinking and girls. They made Belfast on a Saturday night sound like Dawson City. There seemed no reason why this amicable state of affairs should not continue throughout the term, the academic year, the three-year course, even beyond into distant adult life, old acquaintance, auld lang syne. Why not indeed? Joe was why not. They reckoned without Joe and his incorrigible habit of bringing history into everything.

The tea break went well at first. Swimmingly in fact. The word *swimmingly* was all the rage just then among the little group from Flax Spinning. It had been taken up with delight when a poor old Englishman who taught mechanics had used it innocently when enquiring about the progress of an experiment involving swinging balls. And our swinging balls? Ah yes, swimmingly, swimmingly. As the group sat down they addressed to each other the Belfast demotic greeting 'what about ye' as coarsely as possible to which the answer was 'oh swimmingly, swimmingly. And your swinging balls?'

They talked loudly above the chatter all around them. Exams. Girls. Dance halls. The Cotton Denier system of yarn measurement. The bloody awful Mechanics paper in Part 1. Who that sexy voiced girl was on the switchboard of York Street Mill.

Henderson the Catholic spoke of the Old Girls' party at St Malachy's. Kathleen ... used to be hockey captain ... not a bad looker ... tits well handled *but* ... you know ... awful big mouth, voice that carried ... sudden hush when record jammed ... Kathleen's voice ... teachers, mothers ... *If you're trying to find out whether I'm a virgin well I* AM ... bloody man didn't know where to put his face!

Harry said that old Gummy who worked the yarn baler at Taylor's had told him that the wet spinners used to catch hold of a lad that had just started, pull the trousers off him and then do something awful to him with a lump

176

of tow dipped in some concoction. Harry imitated old
Gummy's slow lugubrious speech. The older women weren't
too bad but some of them young hussies wouldn't know
that part of a man is delicate.

What was the finest linen yarn, somebody asked, and
Henderson said at York Street it was one hundred LEA.
But that was nowadays, they objected. Used to be one
hundred and fifty. Ladies' linen shifts. Don't wear them
any more. That switchboard girl sounded as if she didn't
wear them! Joe said the finest yarn ever made was three
hundred LEA which was greeted with astonishment and
incredulity. Where? Get away! Not in a bloody Belfast
mill. Never! Joe said no, it was in ancient Egypt. Some
mummies had bandages made from linen yarn as fine as
human hair. Spun with a distaff, not even a spinning
wheel. They speculated eagerly on how this could have
been done. There seemed nothing to disrupt the perfect
harmony that prevailed. Egypt under the Pharaohs is
hardly a minefield through which mixed company would
have to step with care and not even Joe tripped over a
booby trap there. When Henderson said they should have
a look at the mummy in Belfast museum and Joe said,
no, it was only the Pharaohs that were wrapped in the
fine linen and he did not think that Belfast would have
got hold of a Pharaoh, they all had a good laugh at the
idea of Belfast getting a Pharaoh and there was unanimous
agreement that a Belfast mummy would have been somebody
that had 'come up from nothin' that the daughters could
take nowhere. All went swimmingly in fact. Harry even
got a little more mileage out of swinging distaffs and
swinging balls though complaining bitterly about the bloody
awful Mechanics paper in Part 1. Somebody sighed wearily
$v = gt^2$. That was where the booby-trap was. In the law
of motion of falling bodies, the velocity is directly
proportional to the square of the time.

Joe said did they know that Galileo was an awful conceited bugger ... this book he had found in Smithfield ... Newton, Kepler, Galileo ... terrible bloody man ... thought nobody could discover anything but himself ... claimed every bloody discovery going ... belittled everybody else ... $v = gt^2$ – yes that was his all right but the bloody telescope no ... had rows with everybody ... nearly makes you sympathise with ... the Catholic ... the Inquisition.

He should have spotted the danger in the name Galileo. He should have shut up immediately he blundered into the words *Catholic* and *Inquisition* and changed the subject to something absolutely innocent like the well-handled tits of St Malachy's or his own church badminton team well groped at the back of the Sunday School hall. Although aware of a sudden chill in the atmosphere he thought to dispel it by plunging on into what he imagined would be a good-and-bad-on-both-sides balancing of the score. Kepler, said Joe, wildly. Protestant Kepler. But lived in Catholic Germany ... protected by the Catholic church as a man of science. Feet were pressing his foot under the table. It made Joe obstinate and angry. Henderson was looking embarrassed and offended. He muttered that there was no call to bring *that* into it. There was something in the way Henderson muttered that seemed to imply that the Inquisition was crude Protestant propaganda. Joe was outraged and reckless.

'Oh for Christ's sake,' said Joe, 'haven't you got a mind of your own?'

Harry put in very hurriedly that the Matric French paper had been harder than the Senior Cert French paper when it was supposed to be easier. They all except Joe eagerly took up the theme of the unfairness of exams that were supposed to be easier not being easier, citing cases of those who had suffered unjustly, but it was the eagerness of strain. Not *swimmingly* any more. Back at the spinning frames in the Textiles department everybody was extra polite to Henderson and the other Catholic to try to make it up to him for the breach in the code that governed good relations between Catholics and Protestants.

Back at Taylor's Mill next day Joe and Harry had a row about it although in fact the anger was all on Joe's side, Harry adopting the more-in-sorrow-than-in-anger stance which made Joe angrier. Harry looked up to Joe and Joe was getting tired of being looked up to by Harry. There had been times before the College canteen incident when Joe had found being looked up to by Harry a responsibility he did not wish to carry, as it seemed to involve, as now, feelings of moral guilt for letting Harry down. Harry was wearing his disappointed-in-someone-I-looked-up-to look and spoke only brief reproachful phrases in answer to Joe's tirade against *their* bloody priest-ridden education. A bit off-colour, Joe, Henderson not a bad fella. But it's a *fact* of history. Yes, well, but not *their* history, be reasonable. THEIRS! It's bloody *European* bloody history. Yes, well, live and let live... Ah you know.

They conducted this debate in the open air, in the great cobblestoned yard of Taylor's as big as a village square. They paced the elegant arched colonnades along the Counting House. They might have been two philosophers in the Age of Reason, the one listening gravely, the other vehement. Joe would have none of *their* history. He had had enough of *their* this and *their* that. He put on a 'neighbour woman' voice and said, falsetto, 'They have *their* days and we have *ours*'. He mocked a kind of chorus of decent Protestant women like his mother chanting The Articles Of Being Good Neighbours With The Catholics. They have *their* history and we have *ours*. Sure a bit of politeness costs nothing. They have *their* laws of motion and we have *ours*. No call for bigotry at all. They breathe *their* air and we breathe *ours*. They have *their* well known facts and we have *ours.* Sure only a right Shankill Road gaunch that couldn't watch his mouth would bring up Galileo in mixed company!

Their perambulations up and down the colonnade attracted the attention of a group of mill girls who passed by and then stood looking back at them passing remarks and emitting wolf-whistles. A wee courting couple. Having a wee lovers' tiff. Ah go on, kiss and make up. The attentions of the girls worked an unmistakable trans-formation in Harry. Diffident though he might be about history, in need of reassurance about his ability to cope with the stern task of living in all its other departments, about girls he had no fears, no doubts, none whatsoever. He knew with a sure and certain instinct what to do when mill girls wolf-whistled. Joyously he wolf-whistled back. For a moment their roles were reversed and it was Joe who looked up to Harry. He thought wistfully that he would rather be able to do that than know all about Newton, Galileo, history.

They retreated into the Counting House more aware than usual of the Red Hand of Ulster emblazoned above the portals. In the vestibule the large framed picture was in its usual place but this time they stopped at it. It was a yellowing photograph of the mill yard taken at a moment of history. Men mill workers in cloth caps were parading with sloped rifles. An open motor car full of Army officers looked on approvingly. The wheels of the car were turned in such a way as to suggest that it had just then swerved to a stop and would soon be off again to inspect similar musters of Protestant men elsewhere before reporting in high places that Ulster would not have Home Rule, that Ulster would fight and Ulster would be right!

Joe said to Harry did he recognise old Gummy the yarn baler at the end of the back row and Harry said he looked as if the spinners had just done that on him with the lump of tow and wasn't it a scream the way he kept

180

his teeth in his lunch box. Joe said did he never show you his Blighty One. The wound that saved his life. Like a zip fastener round his middle. A machine gun bullet. Only three of the men on the picture came back. The Ulster Volunteers. Joined to fight Home Rule and were marched off to fight the Kaiser instead ... the Somme 1916. That too was History.

15

He began to discover that the literary impulse was more common than he had thought, the chief difference between it and the seemingly more widespread urge to make music or sketch or paint pictures was that unlike them it is not openly acknowledged but kept very private, disclosed only confidentially with great coyness. The first time he became aware of other secret scribblers, it was when a friend of one of his brothers – one of the crowd of tanned and virile mountain ramblers sorting out their rucksacks at the back of the house, their maps, frying pans, their soda-bread and bacon – edged Joe away from the group into the shed, and there, as if it was the most natural thing in the world to do, produced ... a thick manuscript. Something he had scribbled down for a bit of a cod. Not the Great Irish Novel of course, ha, ha. But Joe might like to cast a discerning eye ... not to flash it around. What on earth can I say, Joe wondered dismayed, and his dismay came between him and the pages of close neat handwriting. There seemed to be a great deal of piano playing. At every crisis in the passionate adulterous love affair there was always a piano handy on which the hero could play sad music softly while people spoke their lines. But, Joe thought puzzled, was it not his sister that was taking the music exams? He returned the manuscript trying to make vaguely encouraging noises with sincerity and thereafter avoided being alone with the author.

Then a fellow at work did it. This time the theme was Ireland after the Bomb. The fellow was in Payroll and was taking the Accountancy exams. After the Bomb the main Irish problem was to replenish the empty towns and cities with babies. There was an acute shortage of men not fully explained. Young men were obliged to ... many women. Society became Amazonian ... a fierce creature called Orange Lily ... male stud farms ... almost becomes unit of currency. Yes. Well. Very ... ah ... vivid, said Joe lyingly. When you think of the tripe that gets printed, he added, encouragingly indignant.

He came to recognise the preliminary overtures, the ominous signs, leading up to being taken to one side and a manuscript coyly being produced. It was a little bit like being approached by nancies, in that the overtures would sometimes come from unlikely quarters. Like all youths of slender build who seem particularly to attract homosexual advances Joe had long since learnt to recognise the signals early and to put them off by making it clear that he was *not*. With scribblers this was not so easy since he *was*. Sometimes when someone said that he had heard that Joe ... did a bit in that line himself ... he would say hurriedly that he used to ... just a bit of a phase we go through ... like pimples and wet dreams, ha, ha.

He wondered resentfully how they knew. He didn't go about taking people aside and showing them bloody manuscripts. Like showing your privates. In print would be different. Something about print that covers the bare bum.

Yet he knew well enough how they knew. *Girls*. It was not just the great love of his life whom he had bombarded with passionate love letters larded with quotations, some of which he made up himself. There had since been others. The fact that this policy of wooing working-class girls by correspondence had not been markedly successful had not yet cured him of it even though each time he vowed never again. He was bitter that the girls had flashed his letters about under pretence of being impressed. The

183

latest episode had been particularly painful since he had
written to her after being rejected in circumstances of
cruel irony. She had quoted scripture at him when they
were embracing passionately in a dark alleyway and he
had been moved to speak of love. Love? Oh no! Kisses,
she implied, yes, maybe more. But *love* no! Bewildered
and yet half knowing why he had asked why. Why! And
very distinctly she said 'Be ye not unequally yoked together
with unbelievers'. St Paul. But surely ... both Protestants
... those kisses. But even in his dismay he knew what she
meant. She was a Brethren. Desperately he tried to say
that he ... might come to know the Lord. For the sake
of her kisses and more than kisses. For he had never
been kissed like that before. Had kissed like that. But
been kissed back no. And he was to have no more for
being so foolish as to speak of love? He would write of
love instead. He would quote scripture back at her, not
St Paul, she was too lovely for St Paul. *Rose of Sharon.
Lily of the valleys. Fair as the moon. Lips like a thread of
scarlet. Thy two breasts like two young roes which feed among
the lilies. Thy navel like a round goblet. Honey and milk are
under thy tongue. How fair and how pleasant art though, O
love, for delights!* Song of Solomon. She never replied.

But he could not blame girls for Mr Blair. The Mr Blair
business was because he sent something to a literary
competition he had seen advertised, famous writers to
adjudicate. He won nothing and his entry was not returned.
Months later he got a letter from Mr Blair in Dundonald.
Joe's poem had been passed to him by someone connected
with the competition. Joe went to see him, not without
misgivings, for Mr Blair had written things like 'kindred
spirit' and 'keeping the flame alive in the black North'
which did not augur well. Mr Blair was a retired teacher
of sedentary appearance. Framed degrees and diplomas
covered the walls of his parlour. He was at pains to let

Joe see how busy he was in the cultural life of the city while affecting to complain ruefully of its onerous burdens. *Never volunteer*, he warned Joe with mock sternness, meaning committees, meetings, licking envelopes, seeing to the tea, your life not your own any more. With difficulty he hid his pleasure at them being interrupted by the telephone in the hall and came back shaking his head deploringly. Ruffled feathers! This Bronze Age dig near Ballinderry. Wouldn't believe they're still fighting and backbiting. Whose names to go on the paper to be put up to the Society! He implied that Joe was well out of it. Now where were they? Oh yes this poem of Joe's.

His poem had been written in his Dryden and Pope phase when he had thought the heroic couplet, the paradox, scathing invective, to be the noblest expressions of the human mind. He had felt that his entry to the competition had contained lines Pope and Dryden might have written such as 'When men are scared to look afraid/ It takes a kind of courage to be a coward' even though they were not in fact a heroic couplet, just heroic. Mr Blair addressed Joe's poem as if marking an examination paper in Eng. Lit. An effective use of metaphor here, a very good dying fall there. Mr Blair spoke expertly of cadence, metre, feet, of scanning systems and rhyming schemes. ABBA. ABCA. Here was an interesting ABCBA. Glad to see Joe wasn't one of your modern fellows who would rhyme 'lost' with 'fast' though Ulster's foremost Protestant poet might not agree! Who did he mean, Joe wondered. Percy French? Too long dead. 'Where the Mountains of Mourne sweep down to the sea'. But of course Mr Blair meant none other than our very own Louis MacNeice. Joe murmured 'Sit on your arse for fifty years and hang your hat on a pension', which was the only MacNeice that Joe knew, from hearing his father quote it without knowing where it came from when he spoke against the Dead Hand Of

Old Fogeyism in Church and State. Mr Blair said he was glad to see that Joe was a MacNeice man and hinted at the possibility of meeting the great man. Oh yes. Oh Mr Blair knew Louis, and Mr Blair gave a smile mostly affectionate but hinting that knowing Louis could have its ups and downs. Had sat in that very chair Joe was sitting in not a lifetime ago. The time of the Arts Festival at Queen's. Louis one of the adjudicators. Mr Blair dropped his voice confidentially and said wryly that there were times Louis knew what he was here for, and times he did not. Ireland's scourge. The poets' curse. Joe, he hoped, would keep well clear of the bottle.

Joe had the feeling that all this was leading to something familiar. Even when Mr Blair spoke of *little evenings* that Joe might like to come to – only cocoa he said slyly, we're called the cocoa school – he felt that something else was the main point of the meeting. Mr Blair said that he sometimes 'wooed the muse' himself. Yes. Had to plead guilty. Jotted something down from time to time. Louis had taken something of his away with him ... if he could just lay his hand on it. He made a show of having to search through the drawer of a roll top desk and produced a sheet of paper for Joe to read. Not to take away and read, but read with Mr Blair watching him eagerly. Joe tried to focus his mind upon the typed words laid out neatly in rectangles but all he took in were technicalities like frequent use of 'th'' for 'the' and a profusion of accent marks for the odd stressing of syllables. 'O Woman!' one stanza began which perversely and somewhat cruelly made Joe acutely aware of Mr Blair's little paunch and thinning hair.

He escaped as soon as he could with the best grace he could muster but for a long time he was troubled by the memory of Mr Blair's face watching him read the poem, eagerly soliciting praise. The other scribblers were different. They, like himself, were young. They'd get over it, grow out of it. Mr Blair seemed an object lesson in what happened to people who did not grow out of it, still 'wooing the muse' late in life, 'O Woman!'-ing with a bald patch and a little pot belly, pathetically brazen in their hunger for esteem.

Joe put his latest notebook into a small sack with a brick in it and threw it into the Lagan. He thought he would feel sad about it. Instead he felt relieved and that part of him which had always held that life was for living not describing now urged him to devote himself without further delay to the important things in life. Images occurred to him illustrating what these were, all having to do with being on easy terms with his fellow men and women. That cousin of his father's, for instance, in his canary coloured overcoat, little trilby hat and a fancy woman in Newtownards. That time he had shaken Joe's hand with a firm grip in which there was a pound note and in such a way as to make refusing it an impossibility. It took a thousand years of civilisation to produce a gesture like that and Joe wondered in admiration and despair if he would ever master the art of it.

There was much talk at the time of the young people these days going through phases. Not like the old days, the people said wonderingly, you daren't have a phase in the old days or they would have dosed you with castor oil. His aunts spoke of some of his cousins and their phases. With Anna it was the stage. Prancing about in some seaside hall half-naked in a grass skirt, that boyfriend of hers with the patent shoes and the wee moustache. She'll grow out of it. With Barbara it was the horses. If she's not riding them she's forking out manure down at the stables. Can't get the smell out of her clothes. But it's just a phase. When she takes up with somebody she'll stop smelling like that. *He'll* stop her smelling like that!

The idea of youth being a time for the trying on of guises, most of them unsuitable, appealed to him. Sometimes he wondered if his whole life since passing the scholarship had not been a guise that did not suit him. Boyhood had suited him. He had known who he was then, notwithstanding being a dreaming boy living half in books. His brothers and their crowd had their ball games, their camping and mountaineering to form social bridges that allowed easy crossing into the middle class, easy maintaining of old connections that lay behind. He was bridgeless. He no longer belonged. He was *outside.*

For a time he was invited to a large untidy house in the Malone area, full of sports gear, books, noisy extrovert family life, invaded by crowds of young people all dauntingly good-looking and articulate, cheerfully insulting each other with a freedom he was invited to participate in, but could not. He had met one of the sons in hospital when they both had their tonsils out and had been the only adults in a children's ward. The family spent summer weekends at an old farmhouse in the Antrim hills where a stream was dammed to form a bathing pool. They invited Joe and crowds of others. People would have to take pot luck they warned, you might get a bit of straw to lie on and you might not. Good for the soul. He cycled out along the Coast Road past Larne before turning up into the heather. It was a brilliant day with the sea on one side and the white cliffs on the other. He thought how little he had seen of his native land and how beautiful it was. Slemish Mountain was in the distance, a vivid slab, and the sky was blue.

When he reached the farmhouse it was deserted though littered with unmistakable signs of their presence. Shouts and splashes came from down the hill. They were at the pool. There was a typewriter on a table in the main room that still had the iron crane for the potato pot over the huge open fireplace. There were piles of papers. Somebody was marking exam papers. Choice bits would be read out for them all to hoot with laughter at. Here's a fellow thinks the French for cup of tea is *coup de thé* I suppose he thinks that *coup de grâce* is to do with communion wine or some kind of ice cream concoction! In one of the outhouses there were sleeping bags. He opened the door of what might have been a byre to reveal little heaps of girls' clothing. He lay on the grass and looked down upon them disporting around the pool. Some kind of ball game was being played in which scoring a goal was marked by throwing whoever had failed to stop it into the pool. The older people umpired the game in white floppy hats to keep off the sun. He watched as young men of admirable physique seized a pretty girl in a swimsuit and hurled her shrieking into the water. It seemed to be part of the fun to pitch her in headlong. A graceful girl, they flung her in graceless. He turned away. His physique was not admirable enough. He rode off without disclosing his presence. He had seemed to have glimpsed an Eden that he could not enter. It made him suddenly heartsick for what now seemed that other Eden which had once been his and from which he had been long expelled. The way those athletic young men at the pool casually laid hands upon those beautiful young women with no thought of doing anything out of the ordinary prompted the memory of that now distant time when he had been a smiling boy lording it over the girls of The Free School, taking it as no more than his due when they accused each other hotly of loving him and chalked his name in their love circles in which it was stated categorically that maidens loved him.

As he cycled back through Belfast in the late summer evening he felt a great need to replenish his soul with something from its sources in the rich rough culture of the streets. The drumming of his wheels upon the stone square sets suggested where he might find a taste of it. Harry's garage. Although it was Saturday evening Harry's might still be not quite shut. When he reached it, only half of the big door had been brought across the entrance. The closing of Harry's garage was, like the northern twilight, a long gradual affair. Harry was spinning a motorcycle wheel mounted on the bench and doing something to the spokes, watched by two men. He sometimes plucked at the spokes and listened so that he seemed to be playing a harp. Joe went into the little office and sat down on one of several old motor car seats. Harry was used to people just wandering in and sitting down. Various musical instruments were lying around. Joe took up a mandolin and after hunting down a plectrum in Harry's desk picked out 'Drink to me only with thine eyes' very slowly with long pauses between notes. The instruments were there for all sorts of reasons: for repair; for sale; or simply being 'minded' for someone. Sometimes people who wandered into Harry's could play one or more of the instruments.

One of the men talking to Harry as he deftly tuned the motorcycle wheel came into the office and sat down, greeting Joe by name. He had been a labourer for Mr Laffin the time Joe kept the books and was a flute player in an Orange band. Joe remembered with affection his lively mind, avid for startling facts about the physical world or the human condition for which he scanned the papers eagerly at the tea breaks while the others studied the horses. He had not changed. He picked up a Sunday newspaper lying on a car seat and after a time read aloud several items of a sensational believe-it-or-not kind. He had been to England and had acquired a half-cockney accent which quite suited his slight cock-sparrow frame and cheerful gleaning of the crumbs of knowledge. Eighty-

190

year-old woman in Peru gives birth. Bishop says Darwin right. Surgeons remove live goldfish from solicitor's gullet. Reckoned to be five thousand million suns in universe. Crippen innocent, fresh evidence. It makes you think, he said eagerly to Joe. Then he examined a large wooden wind instrument, probably left there by some schoolchild waiting at Harry's for the mother. He tootled runs of notes on it very skilfully before playing a piece that was sweet and yet majestic, filling the little room with stately elegance. Joe asked him what it was and he said it was Handel, a minuet. The sound of it brought in his friend, who took down an accordion from a shelf and tried to follow him on it wherever he could. But the accordion being less suited to classical music they changed to playing military marches; dance tunes; the airs of songs. Harry was seen closing the other half of the big street doors though he kept the small panel door open and stood at it for a time surveying the street, still reluctant to shut it out completely. Then he closed it too and came into the office where he began tuning a violin to suit the other instruments, though without stopping the music. Harry had thick stubby fingers that came down on the strings with a perceptible thump yet the notes were beautifully true.

They played the old song tunes that Joe loved; the rag-time tunes, Victorian drawing-room ballads and music-hall songs that his father had sung round the house or in his workshop. The songs were wordless yet the words hung in the air just the same. *Left me all alone-ee-oh, oh my Antonio ... She's no girl for sitting down to dream, she's the only Queen Laguna knows ... I'm the man who broke the bank at Monte Carlo.*

They had to stop playing for a few minutes when the public houses closed. A group of passing men knocked on the doors attracted by the sound of the music, the euphoria of the glittering bars, though fading, still upon them, reluctant to believe that the Belfast Saturday night had no more to offer than home and a wifely bed. They could bring in drink, they called. They knew where they could get a crate of stout, they cajoled enticingly. But Harry put them off through the closed door. Was going home that minute. Just as soon as he could get closed. When the last of the steps died away they resumed playing.

Joe's only part was that of avid listener. He knew quite well that it was old-fashioned of him, that he should really prefer jazz, swing, the latest hits on the radio and on films that young people all over the city at that very moment were listening to, dancing to. The old music-hall songs belonged to an age that was dead and gone before he was born. Yet he heard in them something that refreshed his soul at its deep roots back in the rough rich culture of the urban Protestant working class and made him think of the *Titanic, Pilgrim's Progress*, public houses, the Bible, Robbie Burns, Gospel Hall hymns; his father's old uncle speak of hearing Charles Dickens read 'The Death of Little Nell' in the old Linen Hall. These and other images soothed his wounded spirit with their healing balm.

The last thing they played before Harry definitely closed was 'Bye Bye Blackbird'.

> Where somebody waits for me,
> Sugar's sweet, so is she,
> Bye Bye, Blackbird.

16

There was a time when big shoe-shops in Belfast had journeymen shoemakers making stock sizes for the shelf as well as bespoke. If people mentioned such things with a sigh of regret when they gathered at the weddings that were now occurring so frequently among Joe's cousins, the sigh was not for the passing of handmade shoes, about which they cared nothing, but because that was when they were in their prime and all the things they might have done with their lives were still there to do. When a bride and groom went by air to Canada after the reception people said that this flying was a marvel and recalled the times when the big ocean liners called at Belfast on the way to America and were a week on the water. Joe heard yet again the story of how he had once got lost on an Atlantic liner the time they saw his Uncle Billy off to New York.

Why did he not remember getting lost on the great liner? He remembered something of the ride to the docks, them all piled into taxis, of going onto the boat he thought was the liner it was so big but it was only the tender that took them out to where the liner was in Belfast Lough. Yet of boarding the liner and wandering off he could only hear as if it were a story of someone else – the liner scoured from top to bottom, his mother in a state and such a description of her he gave the sailors as well she didn't know it at the time! His memory stopped short of that. Perhaps that was because, like all lost child episodes it had been appropriated by his mother as *her* experience, not his, perhaps not without a struggle, now forgotten, in which he had resentfully let go. He listened absently to them recalling such fond times. He tried to work out without asking them when that time was when he had been a lost child on an Atlantic liner. There was something in the news around that time that the people were all talking about. Ghandi and his goat? No. Munich? No. The *Thetis* submarine disaster? No. The Spanish Civil War or was it the Japanese in China? The people running from the bombs on the news in the Picture House (was that Shanghai or Spain?) soldiers on a beach triumphantly hailing the sea (were they Franco's?) and himself being shushed angrily for asking were they the good ones or the bad ones? The Jubilee? The Coronation? The Coronation mug with only one head on it? Yes. Edward and Mrs Simpson. The time Billy went to New York and was a week on the water. *Wore plus fours on a Sunday that would be Mrs Simpson the oul' father very strict and hard on him* and Joe's mother and his aunt at the wireless, crying (would that have been the woman-I-love abdication speech?).

He remembered the deck of the tender and the wind on his face in Belfast Lough; the stern sense of purpose that ennobles motion on water; people in tears waving; the singing of some farewell song with Ireland in it; the grey sky, the grey sea, the crying gulls; the huge black cliff with the portholes in it towering over them and whatever lay beyond.

Australia. South Africa. Canada. New Zealand. Everybody knew people who had gone or were on the way or were about to sail or who were waiting for the tickets or who had filled in the papers. People spoke familiarly of the names of cities in distant lands, of the names of shipping lines and ships, of the bum-boats that crowded round your ship at Port Said.

A man where he worked had a spare set of immigration papers which, half idly, he filled in and sent off. In answer to the question what friends had he there he put *none*, and where it asked what city did he want to go to, he put *any*. Here is a fellow of spirit, they would say admiringly when they read what he had filled in.

He was summoned for an interview to a small office up some stairs in Glengall Street. The man had a colonial accent all right but seemed neither sun-tanned nor virile. Am I doing the right thing? Joe wondered.

Let me give you a piece of advice, the man said. Ah, Joe thought, so, sallow and sedentary though the man seemed, he had perhaps been impressed by the boldness of 'any' city and friends 'none'.

Never, the man exhorted him, enclose a stamped addressed envelope to a government department.

Six men were waiting their turn on the stairs when he came out. Was it too late to turn back? he wondered. The man had a little rubber stamp which he brought down decisively like an auctioneer's hammer on the application papers upon which he could see his own writing the way we would see our writing in an old school book, evoking the memory of a former time. Going, Going, Gone, went the little stamp.

In the months that followed his interview with the immigration man the wheels that he had set in motion so impulsively ground remorselessly on. He would hear with a pang of dismay people refer lightly to some future event when he would be gone. Never had the streets and roads been so dear to him, and there were trees too, trees that were dear old friends: he knew with certainty that they would chop them down when he was gone.

When the travel papers came it was summer. Never

had a summer seemed so full of friendliness and laughter. He discovered for the first time the pleasures of standing with the fellows at the corner and whistling after the passing girls. One of the fellows could play the mouth organ and some of them could sing.

> On top of Old Smoky all covered in snow
> I lost my true lover through courting too slow.

They sang softly in harmony, accompanied by the plaintive mouth-organ. The brilliant evening sun lit up the hills between the houses at the end of the street. They spoke of the big fight, about women; the Sunday gambling schools; whether a drink of water the morning after could make you drunk again; whether the male could be locked to the female in the act of copulation, requiring medical intervention; whether the rhythm in the fox-trot was slow, slow, quick, quick, slow. It almost seemed as if he had learned at last, when it was too late, the knack of being a happy idle sauntering fellow on easy terms with all.

One of the places that would cost him more than a pang of regret to say farewell to was Belfast's principal centre of learning, namely the arcade of second-hand bookshops in Smithfield which had long been a refuge from the noise and bustle of the city, and perhaps – for those who succumb early to the lure of browsing silently in books – from much else besides. He had long been a frequenter of the bookstalls and the melancholy thought sometimes occurred to him that life was passing him by. *Lingering by the bookstalls of Smithfield while life passed him by* was actually the form in which the thought occurred to him and the words seemed to have a pleasing cadence. Am I a poet then, he wondered, is that what I am? Sometimes on the way to Smithfield he would stop at a shop window in which a certain arrangement of mirrors gave back an unfamiliar reflection of himself seen from the side. Is that what I seem to others, he would wonder, sometimes with dismay, sometimes with vanity, always with awe at its strangeness. Not always when he arrived at the bookshops had he fully set out to go there, especially on Saturday afternoons when he might sally forth into the city vaguely hopeful of adventures more substantial than those of the mind, yet often turning at last with a feeling in which there was relief as well as defeat into Smithfield's cobble-stoned arcades in which life moved in the pages of old books.

Not long before he sailed he looked among his books and picked two to take with him. One was a Biographical Dictionary. It gave him pleasure to dip into it because of being able to hold in his hand, as it were, brief lives of all the famous people who had ever lived, from Aagsen to Zwingli, but only up to 1899 which was the date it was published, a fact which, while it was certainly a shortcoming, also in some way added to the interest of browsing in it. Lloyd George was a rising young politician; W B Yeats was just coming into notice; Winston Churchill was no more than the son of a famous father; Cecil Rhodes was still alive. He caught thereby a faint glimpse of what the world looked like when his father was young. That, and the thought of all those figures of the twentieth century who were undoubtedly then walking the streets but still unknown, waiting in the wings, as it were, for their turn in the limelight, appealed to him as a kind of innocence as he lay on the grass in the summer sun and fell into a reverie over the echoes that rose from its pages of the times that his father had grown up in.

The other book was *The French Revolution* by Thomas Carlyle. He had not known that there had flocked to Paris then such a multitude of people eager to play a part, some of them poets, reformers, scientists, philosophers,

SAM KEERY

Irish patriots, Americans left over from the War of Independence. He found something deeply moving in the constantly recurring image of these minor figures whom he had vaguely heard of only in some entirely different connection, coming and going, coming and going, as if in some great drama upon a stage, emerging briefly and then vanishing again *into Cimmerian night*. He was at the same time fascinated at the idea of all those lives that had left a trace behind them even if only for a brief illuminated moment or two. He came across the name of Paul Jones, the dashing American sailor who had given his name to a dance and fought the British Navy in Belfast Lough, so daring and romantic. Here he was in Paris, no longer romantic. *In faded naval uniform, Paul Jones lingers visible here ... Poor Paul! hunger and dispiritment track thy sinking footsteps: once, or at most twice, in this Revolution-tumult the figure of thee emerges; mute, ghost-like ... And then, when the light is gone quite out ... 'ceremonial funeral' ... Such world lay beyond the Promontory of St Bees.*

In the month that passed before he sailed his head was full of images from Carlyle. As he walked about the streets and roamed the quiet roads his head was full of them. He once or twice tried to tell others what he felt but he had no gift for it. It was like trying to tell not just about a haunting tune but about the sound of an orchestra playing it. It was the chapter titles that had first caught his fancy as he leafed through the pages of the very old edition in Smithfield. It was at the bargain stall where the woman wore a money satchel like a bus conductor and would rattle it from time to time to remind the silent browsers that the books were in fact for sale, some for modest sums, the stall from which men would come away in triumph with perhaps an encyclopaedia as good as new in which there would be depicted as marvels of modern technology the main retort hall of Birmingham gas works or the ship's wireless to which the message was flashed to arrest Crippen the murderer. The chapter titles were like fanfares and proclamations. 'Broglie the War-God'. 'As in the Age of Gold'. 'Sword of Sharpness'. 'Rushing down'. 'Flame Picture'. 'The Gods are athirst'. 'Lion not dead'. 'Lion sprawling its last'. 'The Whiff of Grapeshot'.

He had never read history like that before, not even when he was full of that nonsense of his great epic novel that he was going to write for his great epic love as a means of restoring him to her grace. The French Revolution made him think of history as Art and moreover, art that was superior to the story-telling of novels, more exciting, more tragic, more dramatic, more melodramatic even. He wondered why that was. Was it only romantic fancy? The thought occurred to him that history, like mountains, can be seen whole only from afar. Is therefore, the pathos and drama of history any more a romantic illusion than the blueness and grandeur of mountains which are blue only to a distant viewer but grey and bleak to be among?

One evening as he cycled along a quiet road high above the city he thought he had confirmation of that idea. It was dusk and the dark shape of the city below sparkled with lights. Its beauty touched his heart. Yet it could be seen like that only from a distance, like the blueness of mountains, like the unrolling of the story of the past. He was quite excited by this idea. He hoped it was his own and not something he had read. He tried to think of people he might try it on but failed to imagine a situation in which an opportunity might occur.

That night he dreamed of a great weight pressing down on him, threatening to suffocate him. In the dream he was in a crowded room where people in eighteenth-century costume came and went quite cheerfully, some with familiar faces, but the room was also in some way his coffin and the door its lid, so that he had constantly to remind people not to close the door or he would be buried alive. Some seemed to understand his predicament and complied sympathetically, others he had to shout at angrily. The ones who were sympathetic said of the others that some people were the bloody limit. No consideration nowadays, they said, reverence and solemnity were things of the past. He awoke to find *The French Revolution* lying on his chest.

What would the voyage be like, he wondered. How ordinary the tickets looked, just like any other tickets. Could he not get out of going? Could he just not go? Was it too late not to go? But it was. It had long been too late.

Belfast, like a sky of orange-coloured stars, had glittered in the clear night air and when the early mill horns blew he heard them with sad regret as the voices of departing friends.